ROCCO

LANTERN BEACH BLACKOUT: THE NEW RECRUITS BOOK 1

CHRISTY BARRITT

Copyright © 2021 by Christy Barritt

All rights reserved.

No part of this book may be reproduced in any form or by any electronic or mechanical means, including information storage and retrieval systems, without written permission from the author, except for the use of brief quotations in a book review.

COMPLETE BOOK LIST

Squeaky Clean Mysteries:
#1 Hazardous Duty
#2 Suspicious Minds
#2.5 It Came Upon a Midnight Crime (novella)
#3 Organized Grime
#4 Dirty Deeds
#5 The Scum of All Fears
#6 To Love, Honor and Perish
#7 Mucky Streak
#8 Foul Play
#9 Broom & Gloom
#10 Dust and Obey
#11 Thrill Squeaker
#11.5 Swept Away (novella)

#12 Cunning Attractions
#13 Cold Case: Clean Getaway
#14 Cold Case: Clean Sweep
#15 Cold Case: Clean Break
#16 Cleans to an End
While You Were Sweeping, A Riley Thomas Spinoff

The Sierra Files:
#1 Pounced
#2 Hunted
#3 Pranced
#4 Rattled

The Gabby St. Claire Diaries (a Tween Mystery series):
The Curtain Call Caper
The Disappearing Dog Dilemma
The Bungled Bike Burglaries

The Worst Detective Ever
#1 Ready to Fumble
#2 Reign of Error
#3 Safety in Blunders
#4 Join the Flub

#5 Blooper Freak
#6 Flaw Abiding Citizen
#7 Gaffe Out Loud
#8 Joke and Dagger
#9 Wreck the Halls
#10 Glitch and Famous

Raven Remington
Relentless 1
Relentless 2 (coming soon)

Holly Anna Paladin Mysteries:
#1 Random Acts of Murder
#2 Random Acts of Deceit
#2.5 Random Acts of Scrooge
#3 Random Acts of Malice
#4 Random Acts of Greed
#5 Random Acts of Fraud
#6 Random Acts of Outrage
#7 Random Acts of Iniquity

Lantern Beach Mysteries
#1 Hidden Currents
#2 Flood Watch
#3 Storm Surge

#4 Dangerous Waters
#5 Perilous Riptide
#6 Deadly Undertow

Lantern Beach Romantic Suspense
Tides of Deception
Shadow of Intrigue
Storm of Doubt
Winds of Danger
Rains of Remorse
Torrents of Fear

Lantern Beach P.D.
On the Lookout
Attempt to Locate
First Degree Murder
Dead on Arrival
Plan of Action

Lantern Beach Escape
Afterglow (a novelette)

Lantern Beach Blackout
Dark Water
Safe Harbor
Ripple Effect

Rising Tide

Lantern Beach Guardians
Hide and Seek
Shock and Awe
Safe and Sound

Crime á la Mode
Deadman's Float
Milkshake Up
Bomb Pop Threat
Banana Split Personalities

The Sidekick's Survival Guide
The Art of Eavesdropping
The Perks of Meddling
The Exercise of Interfering
The Practice of Prying
The Skill of Snooping
The Craft of Being Covert

Saltwater Cowboys
Saltwater Cowboy
Breakwater Protector
Cape Corral Keeper
Seagrass Secrets

Driftwood Danger

Carolina Moon Series
Home Before Dark
Gone By Dark
Wait Until Dark
Light the Dark
Taken By Dark

Suburban Sleuth Mysteries:
Death of the Couch Potato's Wife

Fog Lake Suspense:
Edge of Peril
Margin of Error
Brink of Danger
Line of Duty

Cape Thomas Series:
Dubiosity
Disillusioned
Distorted

Standalone Romantic Mystery:
The Good Girl

Suspense:
- Imperfect
- The Wrecking

Sweet Christmas Novella:
- Home to Chestnut Grove

Standalone Romantic-Suspense:
- Keeping Guard
- The Last Target
- Race Against Time
- Ricochet
- Key Witness
- Lifeline
- High-Stakes Holiday Reunion
- Desperate Measures
- Hidden Agenda
- Mountain Hideaway
- Dark Harbor
- Shadow of Suspicion
- The Baby Assignment
- The Cradle Conspiracy
- Trained to Defend
- Mountain Survival

Nonfiction:

Characters in the Kitchen

Changed: True Stories of Finding God through Christian Music (out of print)

The Novel in Me: The Beginner's Guide to Writing and Publishing a Novel (out of print)

CHAPTER ONE

ROCCO FOSTER CROUCHED behind the dumpster, ignoring the scent of decay that rose like the living dead around him. No one could know he and his team were here.

Not yet, at least.

Rocco pressed the button to speak into his tactical communication device. "Everyone in place?"

"Affirmative." Beckett Jones almost sounded bored. That was No-Smile Beckett for you. He sat behind the driver's seat in a van with dark, tinted windows on a lonely street in Norfolk, Virginia. No one should know he was inside and armed.

"Ready to rock and roll." Axel Hendrix was the woman magnet of the group—especially when he rode onto a scene on his motorcycle. He'd been assigned the roof of the four-story warehouse.

"Willing and able." Gabe Michaels, the rookie, was eager to do whatever necessary to prove himself. He crouched on the side of the building opposite Rocco.

They were the team designated for this operation. It should be easy. In and out.

But would it be?

Rocco glanced around the dark urban area again, looking for a sign that their target was approaching. Nothing yet.

"I'm ready to say mission accomplished," Rocco said. "Then we can get some sushi."

Sushi was their thing. It didn't matter how dangerous the team's mission was or how dire their circumstances. Sushi was always their reward—in theory, at least.

Even mentioning it helped break the tension in otherwise life-threatening situations. They'd had plenty of those as former Navy SEALs. But there had been none quite like Operation Grandiose. That one still haunted Rocco. Even sushi couldn't make that dark situation any brighter.

He frowned at the thought of it.

No replays. Whatever happened, no replays.

"Volcano roll for me." Axel's voice broke Rocco out of his somber thoughts.

"Banana roll," Gabe piped in.

Beckett grunted. "You guys are making me hungry."

Hunger was the last thing on Rocco's mind, especially since he had a gun in his hands. He prayed things didn't turn ugly tonight, but he was prepared.

Visionary and entrepreneur Branson Tartus had hired them after he'd found a message on a discarded burner phone in his office indicating an exchange would take place in this location tonight.

One of his employees was trying to sell company secrets, and this person was supposed to meet with an unknown buyer in order to sell the proprietary technology.

The exchange was scheduled to happen at midnight.

Rocco glanced at his watch.

In six minutes.

With each second that ticked by, Rocco's muscles pulled tauter with anticipation.

Performance anxiety?

No.

But adrenaline kept him sharp.

At 11:58, a footstep echoed in the darkness.

"We've got someone approaching the scene," Axel muttered.

Rocco's muscles constricted as he braced himself to act.

Right on cue, a man in black clothing with a dark ball cap pulled low over his face rounded the corner. He took his place by the warehouse door near a broken light.

Just as that message on the burner phone had indicated.

If Rocco had to guess, this guy was the seller. The buyer would most likely show up with money. Possibly with an entourage.

Now they waited for the other party to show up. Then Rocco and his guys would be in business. They'd get the evidence they needed, stop the transaction, and it would be game over.

Easy peasy lemon squeezy, as his mum would say.

Just as the thought went through Rocco's mind, a white van squealed to the curb near the building.

Why would the buyer announce his arrival like that at a secret meeting?

A moment later, a woman hopped from the driver's seat holding a white box in her hands and wearing a bright pink shirt.

Rocco's gaze went back to the van. *Peyton's Pastries* was written in cheerful letters across the side, along with cartoon-like pictures of cupcakes and doughnuts.

Peyton's Pastries? Was that a front organization? If so, they needed to fire whoever had decided this was a good idea.

"Rocco?" Axel clearly sounded confused.

Rocco frowned, his jaw tightening. "Hold steady until I give you the go ahead."

He held his breath as he watched the woman with her dark, curly hair practically bounce toward the man in black.

Rocco braced himself for things to turn ugly.

Then he heard . . . singing.

Singing?

Yes, singing. What was that tune? "Walking on Sunshine"?

Rocco waited for whatever would happen next.

He knew one thing: he needed to be prepared.

For anything.

But especially for the unexpected.

He had already failed the one person in his life who'd meant the most to him.

He vowed never to let that happen again.

PEYTON ELLISON GRIPPED the box of cupcakes to her chest and sang along to herself.

Singing always made her feel better—even if she was terrible at it. That's what everyone told her, but she didn't care.

And feeling better seemed like a great idea right now. This late-night delivery felt so strange—definitely out of the ordinary from her normal cupcake gig.

She studied her surroundings.

This area was so dark. So isolated.

Wasn't this part of town the one that was reported on every evening in the news? An area where crime always took place?

Based on the graffiti bruising the walls, the scent of trash that hadn't been picked up in weeks, and the litter tiptoeing across the ground as the wind ushered it into hiding, Peyton would say yes.

An ominous feeling hung in the air.

This was the perfect place . . . for a crime.

Her steps faltered and she licked her lips, the song she'd been singing disappearing like birthday cake at a party.

Her brother had asked her to come. He'd said he

was at a late-night gathering and that he'd told people how great her cupcakes were. He asked if she could make some so his friends could try them. He'd even added that this part of town wasn't nice but that apartments had been built inside an old warehouse.

She glanced at the old building. These didn't look like apartments to her. Nothing about the area screamed refurbished.

Her instincts told her to run. To flee. To tap into her self-preservation skills.

Then she spotted a man standing by the door, waiting just where her brother had told Peyton to go. Had Anderson sent a friend down to pick up the cupcakes?

Unrest continued to jostle inside her.

The man looked up, and their gazes connected. Peyton couldn't make out his features.

It was too dark. His hat was too low. His collar too high.

He reminded her of someone from an old spy movie—someone who tried to conceal his identity as he met a contact in a shadowy location.

The man's shaded face turned toward her. "Who are you?"

He didn't sound like the cheerful cupcake-seeking influencer she'd imagined.

Peyton held out the box in her hands, her confidence waffling. "I'm here to . . . deliver the goods."

He paused before growling, "Is that right?"

"I think you're really going to love what's inside." She tried to keep her voice light to defuse the tension in the air.

"You have *the goods*?" His voice sounded demanding and unamused. "Open the box."

Anxiety rushed through Peyton. This was not how she thought things would go. But she just wanted to get out of here so she wasn't going to ask any questions and draw this out any longer than necessary.

"Of course." She fumbled with the box top before opening it and revealing . . . two dozen beautifully decorated chocolate cupcakes. Some of her best work. Buttercream frosting. Blue fondant flowers. Candy pearls. Sparkly fairy dust—also known as edible glitter.

She'd worked hard on these only because her brother had made the request.

"What do you think you're doing?" Malice dripped in the man's voice. "There's no money inside."

The man flung his hand and slapped the box.

Peyton gasped as her cupcakes crashed to the ground—the ones she'd spent three hours creating.

They were ruined.

She drew her gaze back up, tempted to give this man a piece of her mind.

But when she saw his bristled shoulders, she knew she was in trouble.

Where was her brother? Why had he asked her to come here? Why had he sent someone else to meet her?

Nothing made sense.

"I . . . I just brought the cupcakes. Like I was told." Peyton's voice trembled as she tried to explain to the man why she was here. But her excuse sounded feeble, even if it was the truth. "But I'll be going now."

The man reached for something at his side.

Peyton gasped when he drew . . . a gun. He pointed it at her, his lips snarling like a rabid animal.

She stepped back, wanting to flee but feeling frozen. "I think there's a misunderstanding here."

"Stop playing games!"

Another round of fear shot through her.

If she didn't make the right move, she had no doubt this moment would be her last. Yet she had so much she still needed to do. So much she needed to prove—not to anyone else. But to herself.

In so many ways, her life felt like it had just begun.

She jerked her head to the side as an SUV raced into view and careened to a stop on the street beside them. The back door opened, and two masked men faced them.

With machine guns in their hands.

CHAPTER TWO

ROCCO HAD no time to waste.

That woman was a civilian. He was certain of it.

He didn't know how she'd been pulled into the middle of this operation.

He'd find that out later.

First, she had to live long enough to explain things.

"Cover me!" he shouted into his comm.

Jamming his gun into his holster, Rocco darted from his spot.

A round of bullets blasted.

Rocco tackled the woman. As they flew through the air, he turned. The woman landed on him instead of on the pavement.

He quickly rolled over her so his body would block any stray bullets.

The woman gasped as she clung to him.

Around him, chaos ensued.

More bullets flew.

People yelled.

The man in black ran.

Too many bullets were flying for his team to go after the guy—not without endangering their own lives.

Rocco didn't want the man to get away.

Yet he couldn't leave this woman.

"Who . . . ? What . . . ?" The woman's voice trembled so badly Rocco could hardly understand her.

"Stay down!" Rocco muttered.

But before anyone could move, another line of machine-gun fire rang out.

The woman whimpered beneath him.

If this continued to escalate, his team might not all get out of here alive.

There was no way he was failing the people most important to him this time.

Absolutely no way.

ALL PEYTON WANTED WAS to crawl under a rock and hide. Or bury herself in cream cheese frosting and a sprinkle of colored sugar.

Instead, she'd have to settle for this bearded giant who hulked over her. He wasn't exactly a rock, but he was close enough.

As another round of bullets flew, she dug her fingers into the man's chest.

He bent toward her, shielding her from anything coming her way. His head was low—low enough that Peyton felt him breathing in her ear. Close enough that she felt his rapid heartbeat against her chest. Close enough that she smelled his leathery aftershave.

Who was this man? Was her earlier guess right? Had she been thrown into some kind of twisted spy scenario like those she saw on TV?

Her heart *pound-pound-pounded* into her chest.

She was going to die, wasn't she?

She would already be dead if not for this man.

Gunfire continued to bombard the air. She buried her head in the man's chest.

Dear Lord, help me!

Tires squealed.

Footsteps scattered.

A smoky scent hung in the air.

Peyton remained frozen. Waiting for something else to happen. Waiting to feel metal pierce her flesh. Waiting for the pain that came with it.

This had to be a dream. A nightmare. She'd wake up soon.

Dear Lord, help me to wake up soon. Please!

The minutes ticked by.

Finally, the man lifted his head and studied her, his brown eyes assessing her for any injuries.

"Are you okay?" A British accent filled his words.

That was unexpected.

Peyton didn't know how to answer, but she *thought* she nodded. She couldn't be certain.

A moment later, he rose to his feet and offered his hand. She reached for him, and his strong grip captured hers. With ease, he pulled her from the ground until she was on her feet.

But as her knees wobbled, she nearly sank back onto the asphalt.

The man caught her elbow and steadied her as he stepped slightly in front of her. He glanced around as if searching for trouble.

This wasn't over yet, was it?

Peyton's trembles tried to consume all her senses.

"We need to get you out of here," the man muttered.

Yes, that was most *definitely* a British accent.

Get her out of here? What did that mean? Peyton needed to get back to her bakery. She needed to make sure her displays were fully stocked for the morning rush tomorrow. She was a night owl and had planned on working into the morning.

Keeping hold of her elbow, the man urged her forward.

But Peyton froze.

Who was this guy? What just happened?

If there was one thing Peyton had learned in life, it was never to move from one bad situation into another.

But wasn't that exactly what was happening right now?

CHAPTER THREE

ROCCO FELT the woman stiffen beneath his grip.

He didn't have time to comfort her or explain.

Those machine-gun-laden men could return at any minute to finish what they'd started.

Besides, the man in black had gotten away.

Not only that, but Rocco's team hadn't gathered any of the evidence they were here seeking.

Unless the person buying this technology was this woman.

But Rocco had never met such a sweet-smelling terrorist before. He just couldn't see this woman being guilty.

One look into her eyes, and all Rocco saw was innocence.

Just then, Axel and Gabe ran toward them,

pausing on either side of them. As Rocco glanced up at them, Axel shook his head.

Rocco knew what that meant.

The gunmen and the man in black had gotten away.

He turned back to the woman. "Listen, I know you're confused. My guys and I will explain everything once we know you're safe. But we need to get you out of here."

She still didn't budge. Instead, her wide, fear-laced eyes studied him. "Who are you even?"

Rocco scanned the area around them for trouble again before his gaze met hers. "My name is Rocco Foster, and I'm part of a private security group known as Blackout. For your safety, you need to come with us."

She took a step back—except Rocco still held her elbow. When he released his grip, she wobbled again.

"I . . . I don't think that's a good idea." Her voice trembled as she spoke. "I should just go to my van. Head into my shop. Work. Keep myself occupied."

He leaned closer. "You don't understand. These people have seen your face. It's not safe. *You're* not safe."

The woman's face paled even more. "What do you mean? I'm a baker. I'm not wrapped up in anything illegal. I just want to go to my bakery. To my apartment. To resume my simple, happy little life—"

They were wasting far too much time here. Rocco's instincts told him that the woman was a Pollyanna. Right now, she was proving that to be true. But Rocco needed to convince her of the danger she was in, and he needed to convince her soon.

"Please." He stooped to meet her gaze and lowered his voice. "I know that you don't know me, and I know it's hard to trust strangers. But at least get in the van with me and let me explain. Otherwise, I'm afraid your guts are going to join your cupcakes all over the asphalt, and I don't think that's something either of us can handle."

He saw a shiver rush through her.

Rocco hadn't wanted to use such a blunt tactic. But she'd left him no choice. He had to get through to her somehow, and the cold, hard truth seemed to be the best way.

Finally, she nodded, and her legs seemed to loosen. With Rocco's guys flanking either side of them, they hurried to the van they'd parked the next street over. Rocco slowed his steps as the woman struggled to keep up.

No doubt, her muscles felt like gelatin. That was to be expected.

He took hold of her elbow again to keep her moving and on her feet.

He watched for trouble as they walked. They both knew the truth—there was a good chance these guys weren't done yet and would come back for more. If so, Rocco and his guys needed to be on guard.

Finally, they reached their black van and slipped inside.

They needed to drive away from this place, just to be safe.

Then Rocco would answer some of this woman's questions.

He hoped she might answer some of his also.

PEYTON COULD HARDLY BREATHE. What was she thinking getting into this van with these men? A van that smelled like gunpowder and testosterone, at that.

As she sat in the back with darkness surrounding

her, staring at four unknown faces, she realized what a mistake she'd just made. This was Safety 101 stuff. *Don't get into vehicles with strangers unless you never want to be seen alive again.*

She backed farther into the corner, as far as she could squeeze.

Every time she closed her eyes, gunfire replayed in her mind. Her ears still rang. Even her teeth hurt, probably from gritting them. She didn't know.

Peyton only knew she was in a bad spot right now. Forget a rock and a hard place. She was between a war and a natural disaster.

How had such an ordinary night ended like this?

The man seated beside her turned to face her. "As I said earlier, I'm Rocco. What's your name?"

She licked her lips, wishing her throat didn't feel so dry. "Peyton."

"Peyton, these are my associates Beckett, Axel, and Junior."

"I prefer Gabe." The baby-faced man gave Rocco a knowing look. "Just because I was playing with GI Joe figures while these guys were fighting in the Middle East, they like to give me a hard time."

Peyton wanted to smile, but she couldn't.

"Do you have any idea what just happened?" Rocco continued as if he didn't hear Junior.

"I almost got killed." Peyton's voice sounded thin, even to her own ears.

Rocco took his black jacket off and draped it over her. She wasn't even that cold. But she craved comfort. Security.

Somehow, he'd known that. And, somehow, the jacket helped. Maybe it was the scent of leathery aftershave that soothed her. Pleasant scents always had that effect on her.

The driver—Beckett—pulled away from the curb, slowly moving from the area.

But Peyton had no idea where they were headed. She could ask. But she didn't.

"Why did you come to this location tonight?" A sliver of streetlight hit Rocco's face, illuminating his strong features and concerned eyes.

"Someone asked me to make a delivery. My brother, actually. I wouldn't have gone out to that area just for anybody. But I wanted to do Anderson a favor."

"Anderson is your brother?"

"Yes, that's right. Anderson Ellison. Why? Was my brother the real target tonight?" She swallowed a gasp as she pictured her brother out there. What if he hadn't been so lucky? What if a bullet had hit him?

Peyton didn't miss how the guys exchanged glances, some type of silent conversation happening as she sat there.

"I don't know," Rocco finally said. "That's what we are trying to figure out."

Her mind continued to race. "Who was that man wearing black? I thought he was a friend of my brother's but..."

Rocco tilted his head, not bothering to hide the fact he was studying her face. "You really don't know who he is?"

"I *clearly* don't know who he is. I *clearly* didn't know anything like this was going to happen."

"Did the man say anything?"

"He asked me to open the box I brought with me, and then he was ticked that there was no money inside. Why would I put money in a cupcake box?"

Rocco let out a grunt.

"Please, can you just take me home?" She shivered and crossed her arms over her chest.

Please, let this be a nightmare. Let me wake up. Let life return to normal. I need more cupcakes in my life right now, not more bullets.

"I don't think that's a good idea." Rocco's voice sounded low now, and his serious undertones only made Peyton's concern heighten.

"Why can't I go home?" Panic tried to bubble to the surface, but she willed herself to remain calm.

"Because that man you met . . . he's seen your face. And you've seen his face. We believe he's dangerous and that he's trying to do business with a terrorist group."

Shock rocked Peyton's system until her lungs tightened and made her feel like she couldn't breathe. "What? All I was doing was delivering cupcakes. None of this makes any sense."

Peyton massaged her temples, trying to get rid of the pounding that had started there. It was no use. Between that and the ringing in her ears, she had the undeniable urge to take some pain reliever and call it a day.

Rocco bent to look her in the eye again. "I know this is a lot to comprehend, and I'm sorry that you found yourself in the middle of things. Obviously, we can't force you to do anything."

"No, you can't." Saying the words gave Peyton a small sense of power in an otherwise helpless situation.

"If you want to go back to your apartment or your bakery, we'll take you," Rocco said. "Or if you'd like us to take you somewhere safe until we can figure out some answers, we can do that too. I highly recommend that second option."

Peyton didn't even have to think about it. "My bakery. I want to go back to my bakery. Please."

The bakery was her safe space. Her happy place. It was what she'd worked so hard to open and had sacrificed so much for.

Rocco stared at her another moment before slowly nodding. "Okay. If that's what you want. Why don't you give me your van keys? I'll have one of my guys drive it back so you don't have to leave it on the street overnight. I don't think you're in any state to drive right now. Am I right?"

He was right about that. Her head was pounding, ringing, *and* spinning.

She sat up and fumbled in her pocket until she snagged her keyring, the one with a stuffed smiley face dangling from it. She handed her keys to Rocco. He gave them to the man sitting up front in the passenger seat—Axel, if Peyton remembered correctly. Peyton quickly rattled off the address to her bakery.

As the driver pulled to the curb, Axel climbed from the van and darted across the street, heading back to her van. Beckett—the man behind the steering wheel—took off a moment later.

Peyton pushed herself deeper into the corner. She pulled the coat up higher around her neck, craving comfort.

Get away. That was all she could think about. She wanted to escape from this craziness surrounding her and cocoon herself somewhere safe.

But even as the thought danced in her head, Peyton knew safety and peace just might be as impossible as baking a tasty cake in only five minutes.

CHAPTER FOUR

ROCCO SENSED PEYTON'S ANXIETY. He knew this had to be hard for her. There was no doubt about that.

But the last thing he wanted was to drop her off at the bakery and leave her to fend for herself.

In fact, he didn't intend on doing that. If Peyton insisted on staying, he'd need to remain in the van outside her place until he knew she was safe.

He glanced at Peyton again as she backed herself as far as possible into the seat.

The woman had no idea what kind of situation she'd just put herself in the middle of.

She'd said her brother had asked her to come. Was *he* the buyer coming to purchase proprietary technology from the man working for Branson?

Rocco didn't like the sound of that.

Even more, if that was true, then her brother had set Peyton up to potentially take a bullet for him tonight. That was messed up.

Rocco didn't want to give the update to his boss. He knew Colton Locke wouldn't be happy when he heard that a supposedly simple operation had turned into this fiasco.

But he had no choice except to tell the truth. As soon as Rocco could, he'd call Colton and explain what had just happened.

It was almost like these people had known Rocco and his guys were coming. They'd been practically waiting for them. As soon as Peyton had walked onto the scene, they'd been ready to act.

That realization made the sense of dread swell inside Rocco even more fiercely.

As they continued down the road, Rocco glanced at Peyton again.

Something about her just seemed so young. So different from him.

Yet they couldn't be more than a couple of years apart in age.

When people had seen the types of things Rocco had, they grew up fast. That was him. He'd seen way too much. Often, he wished he could erase some of those memories.

But Rocco knew they'd stay with him for a long time, whether he liked it or not. Regrets were like that.

Finally, Beckett turned down another street. This still wasn't the best section of Norfolk, but the area was up-and-coming. Little cafés, gift shops, and art galleries were scattered along the historic street that had one time been practically abandoned.

The thought of Peyton being here, especially at night by herself, didn't settle well with him.

Rocco wasn't sure why he felt so protective of this woman he hardly knew. But he did. Maybe it was because he sensed she needed someone to watch her back—especially if her brother had betrayed her. Especially if she wore rose-colored glasses double the prescription strength of anyone he'd ever met.

"It's just up ahead." Peyton's voice sounded fragile, as if it revealed the fear she tried to cover up like icing covering a bland piece of cake.

Beckett pulled the van to the curb. But when Rocco glanced at the building with the sign reading Peyton's Pastries, he did a double-take.

The front window had been smashed.

Based on Peyton's gasp, it hadn't been like this when she'd left.

PEYTON FELT the air leave her lungs as she stared at the bakery she'd worked so hard to open. She'd saved her money, built her business, and had finally opened the doors to this place only six months ago.

The beautiful front window—one she'd paid to have her business name etched on—was now shattered into a million pieces.

She felt like her dreams had been demolished right along with the glass.

She continued to gawk in horror at the sight.

Sure, this was fixable. But the repairs would set her back. Maybe insurance would help, but how long would it take them to make their payout? Peyton would need to hire someone to put wood over the window before thieves broke in and stole any of her equipment.

None of this was even her biggest problem right now.

Her heart pounded furiously in her ears as she remembered the storm of gunfire earlier. The relentless pelting of bullets. The acrid smell of gunpowder. The foreboding sense of danger.

"Peyton?"

She snapped out of her daze and saw Rocco staring at her.

She licked her lips, trying to formulate what to say. There was no one to pick up the pieces for her. She had to pull herself together.

"How did this happen?" she finally asked.

Rocco frowned. "I don't know. But if I had to guess, someone wants to send you a strong message."

"I'd say." Peyton shivered again.

Was this all someone had done? Or had other surprises been left for her inside?

She didn't want to find out.

"What's next?" Rocco's gaze probed hers. "It's your call."

The front passenger door opened.

Peyton shrank back, expecting an intruder to make demands. Maybe even just start shooting.

Instead, Axel hopped into the seat.

She released her breath.

That was right. Axel had driven her van here. With everything that had happened, Peyton had nearly forgotten.

He reached back and handed the keys to Peyton. "I parked your bakery van in the lot behind the building. Hope that's okay."

Peyton thought she nodded and muttered thanks.

But everything blurred around her.

Rocco's question played on repeat in her mind. *What next?*

The idea of going back to her apartment held absolutely no appeal.

There was no way she would have any rest or peace of mind there, not with everything that had happened.

What about her brother? Could she stay with him?

Her brother.

Anderson was supposed to meet her tonight.

So where was he? Was he okay?

Panic raced through Peyton at the thought. How could it have taken her so long to think this through?

What if her brother was a victim here?

Horror reeled through her at the thought.

"Peyton?" Rocco asked.

Her gaze fluttered up to meet his. "I just realized that I haven't talked to my brother. What if these people came after him once we left? What if those men attacked him?"

"Why don't you call him?" Rocco's voice sounded amazingly calm. His gaze locked with hers, almost as if he were using some type of mind trick on her.

A moment of envy passed through her. Peyton had never been that calm.

Her mom used to say that Peyton never walked anywhere. She skipped or ran or bounced. Walking was for the ordinary and the boring, she used to say.

She wanted to smile at the memory, but she couldn't.

With trembling hands, Peyton pulled her cell from her pocket. But her hands shook too badly for her to dial her brother's number.

"Let me help." Rocco's hand covered hers.

Peyton felt a bolt of . . . something . . . rush through her.

Gratitude.

That had been a bolt of *gratitude*. What else could it be?

Because, certainly, at a time like this she wasn't feeling a rush of attraction to anybody.

And if she was, it was simply because the striking man had saved her life. Of *course*, she might have a bit of hero complex toward him after this evening's events.

Peyton rattled off her brother's number, and Rocco dialed for her.

"Is it okay if I put the phone on speaker?" Rocco still held her phone.

"Of course." Peyton didn't have anything to hide, and her brother didn't either.

They were both innocent in all this. They'd been twisted up in an evil plan for reasons other than their own choices.

"Peyton?" Her brother's voice came over the line. "What's going on? You don't usually call this late."

"Anderson!" she rushed. "Where were you?"

"I'm in Detroit. Why?"

"Detroit?" Peyton frowned. That didn't make any sense. "If you're in Detroit, then why did you ask me to meet you tonight?"

"I didn't ask you to meet me anywhere. What are you talking about?"

Peyton shook her head, feeling for a minute like she was losing her mind. "You had your secretary, Suzy, leave me a voicemail asking for two dozen cupcakes. She said you were going to a late-night party in downtown Norfolk with 'movers and shakers' who might be influencers for my business."

"I have no idea what you're talking about, sis." Confusion captured Anderson's tone. "Are you sure the voicemail was from Suzy?"

"She said it was Suzy, and she sounded like Suzy. I didn't exactly double-check. I didn't think it was necessary to call her back."

Anderson let out a long breath. "That's strange. I wish I could help you out with whatever's going on. Maybe someone was messing with you."

Messing with her? Peyton wanted to be mad at her brother. Then again, Anderson didn't know the extent of this evening's events. He was just as much a victim here as she was.

"Someone tried to kill me tonight, Anderson."

"What . . . ?" His voice trailed in disbelief.

"They had machine guns, and . . . I almost died." Peyton swallowed the cry that wanted to escape. This wasn't the time to show her emotions. There would be time for that later.

Just as that thought whipped through her mind, a stray tear trailed down her cheek. She quickly wiped it away before anyone could see.

But she knew it was too late. Rocco had noticed.

"They shot at you? Who would do such a thing? Why?" Anderson asked.

"I have no idea."

"Oh, Peyton. I don't like the sound of this." Anderson's voice hardened, just like it always did when he went into big brother mode. "I'm in Detroit but..."

Peyton knew there was nothing he could do for her—not being so far away. "I'll figure things out."

"Do you want to stay at my place?"

She glanced at Rocco, and he shook his head. She knew what the man was probably thinking. If these guys had tracked her down at her bakery, certainly they could track her down at Anderson's place.

"That's okay," she said. "I'll find somewhere else to stay."

"Maybe with Karen? I'll get there as soon as I can to help you out. I'll try to get the first flight out—"

"Maybe you're better off staying in Detroit," Peyton told him. "Especially if someone purposefully tricked me into going to this location tonight using your name."

"I don't want to leave you alone at a time like this."

Peyton glanced at the men around her. Each wore black. Held guns.

She'd been abducted by the A-Team, hadn't she? That's how she felt, at least.

Right now, they waited for her answer.

"I'll be careful," she finally said.

But there was no way she was staying with Karen. That would only put her friend in danger, and Peyton couldn't do that.

"Are you sure?" Anderson asked. "What happened to you was terrible, and the fact that someone pulled me into this . . . I don't like this. Not at all."

"I'll get it figured out. Really."

Anderson sighed before finally saying, "I'll call you in the morning, okay? I'm so glad you're all right, Pey. I'm sorry this happened to you."

She was sorry it happened too. Going out tonight may not have been one of her smartest moves. Then again, Peyton wasn't always known for making smart moves. She'd rather follow her heart than her head, and that had gotten her into trouble more than once.

"I'll take care of it," she finally said. "I'll keep you updated."

With Anderson's goodbye, Rocco pressed the End button on her phone.

But Peyton's head was spinning with enough force that she felt like she could pass out.

What was going on here?

CHAPTER FIVE

ROCCO SAW the despair on Peyton's face.

He recognized the emotion because he'd lived it.

His heart panged with compassion for the woman and what she was going through.

Was Anderson wrapped up in the scheme?

Rocco didn't know the answer to that. But someone had purposefully lured Peyton out there tonight. There had to be a reason for it.

If Rocco and his team could figure out what that motive was, maybe they could track down the people responsible for the barrage of bullets tonight.

Rocco watched Peyton a moment, observed every emotion that flickered through her gaze. Fear. Confusion. Uncertainty.

He gave Peyton a second to compose herself before asking, "Do you want to go to your friend Karen's place?"

Peyton sucked on her bottom lip a moment, her eyes full of doubt.

The woman was beautiful. No one could deny that.

She had a slender build, expressive eyes, bouncy hair. The contours of her face were even and balanced. Her complexion flawless. Her voice made her seem as sweet as the cupcakes she sold. When he'd thrown her out of the way, he'd gotten a whiff of vanilla. He'd found himself craving more of the scent.

After a moment of thought, Peyton shook her head. "I can't do that to Karen. I'd never forgive myself if something happened to her because of me."

"What's your move then?" Rocco knew what he *hoped* Peyton would say, but he waited for her to draw that conclusion. Whenever he didn't have to force someone to do something, the results were always better.

"I . . ." Peyton shook her head, almost as if she was lost. "I don't know what to do. Should I go to the police?"

"No doubt they're already on their way to the scene. Certainly, someone reported the gunfire." As soon as he said the words, sirens sounded in the distance.

"Were there security cameras? Will the police see me and try to find me? What if I'm a suspect?" Worry swept through her words.

"There were no cameras in that area."

She narrowed her eyes as she stared at him. "How do you know that?"

"Because my team and I checked. If it makes you feel better, maybe you could call the police and give them a statement later—when you're safe."

"And now?" Peyton continued to stare up at Rocco with her big, doe-like eyes.

Rocco swallowed hard, wondering if she ever used those eyes to her advantage.

He felt like putty when he looked into them—and he never felt like putty.

He drew in a breath before saying, "The company we work for has a facility. I'm not going to lie—the place is a decent drive from here. But you would be safe there, at least until we figure out what's going on."

"So I give up everything here and just go to some

strange place to try to figure this out?" Tension formed a knot on her brow.

"You're not safe here." Rocco nodded toward her display window to remind her of the stakes. "I think you know that."

Peyton frowned but didn't argue. After what she'd been through and all she'd seen, how could she?

"Fine." Her voice sounded stiff as her decisive gaze met his. "I'll go. But only because I don't know what else to do."

Rocco heard an edge of desperation to her words. "I think this is the best choice."

"I hope it is." Peyton turned to look out the window, quickly wiping her cheeks.

Rocco knew one thing: this woman was putting her trust in him, and he couldn't let her down.

ROCCO FELT the questions pounding inside him as they headed down the road.

Something wasn't right. Peyton's conversation with her brother had left him unsettled in more than one way.

As miles of countryside and darkness passed,

silence stretched around him. There were some things that he couldn't say—he couldn't take the risk of Peyton overhearing him. But he needed to debrief with his team.

That was going to make for a very long ride tonight.

Peyton leaned her head against the seat, Rocco's jacket pulled over her shoulders. After a few minutes, her weight shifted and her head flopped onto his shoulder. As it did, the sweet scent of vanilla floated toward him.

It reminded him of home. Of shortbread cookies and afternoon tea.

Rocco didn't mind if she used his arm as a pillow. If it helped the woman sleep, then so be it.

But all the questions swirling in his mind made him shift with discomfort. He needed to figure out exactly what was going on. How did Peyton tie into this? Was her brother connected?

What had seemed like a fairly simple assignment had turned into something much bigger.

Even worse, a greedy man could be out there selling proprietary technology to the highest bidder.

For now, Rocco would concentrate on keeping Peyton safe.

In doing so, he hoped they could find some answers and put an end to all this.

But Rocco had a feeling he might have his hands full just with keeping an eye on this feisty, slightly naïve woman.

CHAPTER SIX

PEYTON JOSTLED AWAKE.

She sat up with a start and glanced around.

Where was she?

She was in a van. Darkness hung outside.

And four strange men surrounded her.

But that wasn't what had awakened her.

The tone of the voices around her had changed —as well as the atmosphere.

Something was wrong.

She looked over and saw Rocco sitting stiffly beside her.

Her head rested against his thick arm.

Warmth filled her cheeks when she realized what she was doing. She quickly sat up, muttering an apology as she ran her fingers through her hair. "I'm so sorry. I didn't mean to—"

"It's no problem," Rocco rushed.

But what must the man think of her?

She supposed it didn't matter. There were more urgent matters at hand.

"What's wrong?" Peyton ran a hand through her hair again, trying to shake her grogginess. How could she have fallen asleep at a time like this? Then again, it was the middle of the night.

"We're being followed." Rocco glanced behind them and frowned.

Fear tightened her chest muscles until she felt like she couldn't breathe.

"Just keep your seatbelt on," Rocco said. "We've got this."

We've got this? Who *were* these guys?

Peyton pressed her eyes shut, wishing again that she would wake up from this nightmare. She longed to be back in her bakery with the scents of vanilla and chocolate and buttercream floating around her. With her cheerful icing and sprinkles and other edible candy decorations that made people's days brighter.

She liked living in a world full of happiness and sunshine and flowers.

And cupcakes. She loved living in a world full of cupcakes.

Now she felt as if she'd been thrust into darkness, into a place absent of not only cupcakes, but also sprinkles and sugar.

It wasn't the kind of place she wanted to exist in.

Suddenly, the van swerved to the left.

Peyton gasped.

Before she realized what she was doing, she grabbed Rocco's arm, desperate for something to cling to.

He patted her hand, some of the tension leaving his face as if he wanted to keep her calm. "We've got this," he repeated.

Was that the man's life motto?

She'd heard those words in the past, and they hadn't turned out to be true.

But she pushed those memories down. That was the best place to keep them. Out of sight and mind. Because when the recollections reared their heads, sadness filled her. She worked so hard to let go of that baggage in her life.

"Watch out!" Beckett yelled.

The van swerved again.

Peyton craned her neck as she looked behind her.

But she saw nothing.

That was because the driver behind them remained so close she couldn't even see their headlights.

She slid down in her seat and squeezed her eyes shut again, lifting fervent prayers that they'd get out of this alive.

Then she lifted even more prayers that God would grant her wisdom to figure out which way was up right now.

ROCCO TRIED to conceal his worry. He didn't want Peyton to get worked up. Because dealing with a hysterical woman—or man—on top of being chased by possible assassins?

The two weren't a good combination. Rocco should know. He'd had plenty of missions where he'd had to do just that.

But none of them had ever been on American soil.

He glanced behind him again at the vehicle on their tail. "We need to lose them."

Beckett gripped the wheel. "I'm trying."

The approaching car nudged them.

Peyton gasped beside him but continued to press her eyes closed.

Rocco twisted his neck to see behind them again.

The car had dropped back.

But it wasn't because the driver had decided to leave them alone.

It was the opposite: the driver was revving his engine and preparing for a collision.

Rocco glanced around. They were on a country road. Occasionally, a store, gas station, or old hotel popped up.

But that was all.

They couldn't afford to call the police right now. There was too much that Rocco and his guys couldn't tell authorities. Their mission would raise too many questions.

They needed to handle this on their own if possible.

"It's going to be hard for us to lose them with us in this van and with them in that car." Beckett glanced in the rearview mirror again. "Now, of all times, you guys don't want to give me any advice?"

"Go faster," Rocco said.

Beckett punched the accelerator, and they charged forward.

But the car did the same.

A moment later, it nudged them.

Rocco lurched forward, his seatbelt the only thing holding him in place.

Irritation ripped through him.

They could stop the van, face the people pursuing them, and engage in battle.

But if they stopped, there was a good chance the other car would simply ram them.

Making a sudden choice, Rocco grabbed his gun.

He wouldn't shoot the driver.

But he could shoot out the tires.

He opened the van door, and carefully leveraged himself out the side.

"You sure you know what you're doing?" Axel glanced back for a better look.

"Just keep the van steady!" Rocco aimed his gun.

The next instant, he fired.

And he hit his target.

The car behind them swerved as the driver lost control.

Beckett glanced back at him. "Stop and confront?"

Rocco's jaw hardened before he pulled himself back inside and shook his head. He pulled the door shut and turned to his team. "Any other time, I'd say yes. But not now."

Not with Peyton in the car. They had no idea who was in that vehicle. And if those guys had automatic weapons...

Things could turn too ugly.

Rocco glanced behind him in time to see the car turn off the road.

The driver wouldn't make it much farther on that tire. He must have known that and had given up.

Good.

They were safe... for now.

But how long would that be true?

BY THE TIME the team got to wherever they'd taken Peyton, it was morning. In fact, she'd been able to watch the sun rise as they had ridden over on the ferry.

Despite the harsh situation, a good sunrise always got to her. It was a promise of another new day.

Even though Peyton didn't know what this new day would hold, she was still grateful for it—grateful for the opportunity to make things right, to live her dreams, to help others.

She'd said little since they'd all escaped being

run off the road. There wasn't much she *could* say. And she was *so* tired. She'd drifted off to sleep several times on the ride. The whole thing seemed like a blur.

Finally, they got off the ferry and headed down an old beach road. In between the houses, Peyton caught glimpses of sand dunes on one side. As the contour of the island changed, occasionally she saw water on the other side too.

Rocco had said it was the Pamlico Sound.

Peyton had overheard one of the guys mention that they were on Lantern Beach in North Carolina. She'd heard of this island, but she'd never been here before. However, the setting was breathtaking.

If only she could enjoy it.

They pulled up to a gate surrounded by fencing with sharp wire coils at the top. Someone in the guard station waved them through, and they drove inside.

A few minutes later, they stopped in front of a large three-story building.

"We're here," Rocco said beside her.

Peyton didn't know what to say. Instead, she followed his lead and scooted from the seat. Rocco offered his hand to help her out.

As she slipped her fingers into his, another bolt of electricity rushed through her.

No hero complexes, she reminded herself. This man was doing a job and nothing else.

People who saved your life in a dashing manner were a dime a dozen.

Except they weren't.

To her detriment, Peyton loved warm, fuzzy feelings almost as much as she loved buttercream icing. But she'd learned warm, fuzzy feelings usually led to trouble, just like too many cupcakes generally led to extra inches on her hips and belly.

That was why she primarily made cupcakes for other people and not herself anymore.

She tried to hand Rocco his coat back, but he waved her off. Instead, he helped her pull it over her shoulders. She appreciated it, especially considering the slight chill in the air.

"I'll show you where you'll be staying while you're here." Rocco began walking toward the large building in the distance. "I'm sure you're tired."

"I think I'm getting a second wind." Peyton crossed her arms. "I don't know if I'll be able to rest until some of my questions are answered."

He looked at her long enough to study her face a moment before nodding. "Very well then. That's understandable. But I do need to talk to my boss first. So I'll get you settled and have somebody bring you something to eat. Then we'll meet, and we can discuss things. Give me an hour?"

An hour? She could do that. But any longer and she might lose her mind.

"That sounds fine," she said.

As Rocco led her inside, Peyton wondered just what kind of place she'd agreed to come to.

Things like this weren't supposed to happen to her.

Yet they had.

But the question of why remained.

CHAPTER SEVEN

"IT'S ALMOST like somebody knew we were coming," Rocco told Colton.

He stood in his boss's office with the door closed as he recounted last evening's events. He felt a migraine coming on and needed to take something for it.

They'd been a problem for him . . . ever since Operation Grandiose.

Not now. He rubbed his temples. *Not now.*

He'd have time to deal with his ailments later—when lives weren't in danger.

"That's exactly how it sounds—like this was a setup." Colton frowned from behind his desk, his muscular figure looking out of place in an office environment. "But that doesn't make any sense. The only person who knew we were going to be there tonight was Branson Tartus."

Rocco frowned and stopped pacing for a moment. He'd already thought about that detail. "I know. It *doesn't* make any sense. I can't believe we let the gunmen get away as well as the person selling company secrets."

"It sounds like you didn't have much choice." Colton's jaw tightened, and he tapped his pen on his desk. "Let's investigate some more and then we'll recalibrate."

"Sure thing." But Rocco couldn't let go of last night's events that easily. What happened would stay on his mind until he had answers. Still, he stepped toward the door, knowing he had other things to tend to.

"Listen, one more thing before you go." Colton shifted, the lines on his forehead deepening. "I don't know how to tell you this, so I'll just come right out and say it. Quinn Deblois died yesterday."

The air left Rocco's lungs. Certainly he hadn't heard his friend correctly.

Quinn had been a fellow Navy SEAL. He was a few years older than Rocco, and they'd worked together on several missions.

The man had retired and had been looking

forward to hiking the Appalachian Trail and doing some mountain climbing. He deserved to enjoy himself after all he'd done for this country. He'd put his own life on the line uncountable times.

"Yesterday?" Rocco's muscles went rigid as he turned back to Colton. "How?"

"I just got word of it a few hours ago. Apparently, there was a home invasion, and Quinn was shot. By the time the paramedics arrived, he was already dead."

Rocco shook his head, still unable to process what he had heard. What a tragedy. "I just can't believe this happened."

"I know." Colton's voice remained mellow. "We've all been trying to come to terms with it."

"Are you sure it was a home invasion?" Rocco's mind still raced.

"That's what the police are calling it. Apparently, a few pieces of jewelry and some cash were missing. There have been a series of other burglaries in the area."

"But I know Quinn. Not many people could take him out that easily."

Quinn had been one of the brightest SEALs Rocco had worked with. He'd had great instincts—

not to mention the fact his tactical skills were unrivaled.

As soon as Rocco saw Colton's jaw tighten, he knew his friend felt the same way.

"You think this is suspicious too, don't you?" Rocco pressed.

"I knew Quinn too." Colton sighed, and his gaze darkened as his thoughts seemed to churn inside him. "He was smart, and he was sharp. I used to joke with him and say he faked sleeping at night because no one could ever catch him off guard, not even Axel when he tried to play those stupid tricks on us."

Axel and his stupid tricks. It was hard to believe Quinn wouldn't be around anymore to be on the receiving end of the pranks.

Rocco shook his head, still in disbelief. "So the police are investigating his death?"

"That's right. I'll tell you as soon as I hear anything."

"Do that. Please." Rocco glanced back at the door and the hallway beyond. "Now, I need to go talk to Peyton. I didn't intend to pull her into this, but I couldn't leave her by herself either. I'm sorry for bringing her here without getting clearance first."

"You did the right thing. Hopefully, you can convince her that being here is best until we know something. Plus, she was obviously brought into this for some purpose. We need to figure out why."

Rocco agreed with his assessment 100 percent. "I'm on it. I'll see what I can do."

PEYTON GLANCED around her temporary home. It was too bad she was here out of necessity because her accommodations were totally vacation worthy.

From her second-story window, she had an amazing view of the Pamlico Sound. Even though the sun rose on the other side of the island, the colors it brought were smeared on this side of the island too. Calming pinks and oranges mixed with a touch of purple.

She could get used to this view.

The space was comfortable also. There was a living room, full kitchen, and dining area on one side of the apartment. On the other side was a bathroom, a closet, and queen-sized bed in the bedroom.

Someone had brought her a breakfast sandwich and fruit to eat, along with a mug of coffee and some bottled water. Peyton had attempted to eat, but everything seemed tasteless.

She'd found a bag of clothes outside her door as

well, filled with some yoga pants, casual shirts, and a few other items.

She'd called her two employees to let them know not to come in today and that she was okay.

She'd taken a quick shower, trying to wash away the memories of what had happened last evening.

It was no use. The terror she'd felt was imprinted on her like a permanent tattoo she'd never be rid of.

With those things done, she now paced and waited.

The longer she waited to talk to Rocco, the more her adrenaline faded. But she couldn't rest, not with everything on her mind.

The more time that went by, the more questions she had. The more she doubted her quick decision to stay here.

Maybe she should have thought things through a little bit more. After all, she was in a strange place with people she'd just met. She had only the contents of her wallet, her cell phone, and the clothes she'd worn last night.

Finally, a knock sounded at the apartment door.

Peyton rushed toward the door and threw it open.

Rocco stood there.

Seeing the man took Peyton's breath away, especially in the daylight. He was even more handsome than Peyton remembered.

Not that it mattered.

At all.

She didn't even like beards on guys. But Rocco's . . . it looked *fine*.

Just like he did.

Peyton swallowed hard, wondering where these thoughts were coming from.

Rocco stared at her a moment. When she didn't say anything, he finally asked, "Can I come in?"

Peyton snapped back to reality, realizing she'd been gawking.

"Of course." Her voice sounded scratchier than she would have liked.

Quickly, she stepped aside so he could pass. She really hoped the man hadn't been able to read her expression—and, in return, her thoughts.

She glanced at the apartment and wished she'd cleaned up more. Even though she'd only been here an hour, the leftovers from her meal still remained on the coffee table, a towel on the couch, and all her coffee fixings on an end table.

Being neat had never been her forte.

"Do you mind if we sit?" Rocco nodded toward the couch, not seeming to notice her messiness.

"Of course." She quickly gathered the trash from the coffee table and dumped it on the kitchen counter.

Rocco sat on one side of the couch and Peyton on the other. Then she waited for him to start.

She couldn't imagine what he was about to say.

But anticipation thrummed in her ears as she waited for the answers she so desperately desired.

CHAPTER EIGHT

"WHO ARE YOU GUYS? Are you mercenaries or something? You're like the A-Team, right?" Peyton stared at him from across the couch, her eyes wide with questions.

Rocco held back a smile at the pop culture reference. "Not exactly. We're actually former Navy SEALs."

Peyton looked him up and down before squinting at him. "You don't look or sound like a SEAL."

"And what do SEALs look like exactly?" This would be interesting...

She was quiet a moment before shrugging. "Like the rest of the guys on your team, I guess."

Most tactical guys liked cargo pants, T-shirts, and

boots. Rocco happened to have a more refined style that had been ingrained in him by his British mother.

He rubbed a hand down his beard—one he took pride in keeping neat. No scraggly messes of unkempt hair would be stretching across his cheeks and chin.

"I guess we come in all shapes and sizes," he said.

A sparkle lit her gaze. "I guess you do. So you're former SEALs, and you just happened to be out there last night when all those gunshots started?"

"We were on a mission. An exchange was about to go down."

She shifted, her eyes narrowing. "An exchange? Like . . . a cookie exchange?"

He let out an uncertain grunt. "Just a little different. Someone was trying to sell technology."

"You're going to have to break that down for me. All I can picture is someone selling a used iPhone from an online listing. But this is obviously bigger than that."

Rocco drew in a quick breath, wondering how much to say. The woman deserved an explanation after everything she'd been through. But he knew the truth might not make her feel any better.

"Someone is trying to sell technology developed

by someone else, probably in an effort to get rich quick," he said. "The buyer must have caught wind of what was going down. That's why they opened fire. They thought you were probably a plant or another buyer."

"So that's why he mentioned money..."

"Unfortunately, yes."

"You have no idea who he was?"

Rocco shook his head. "Not really. We were hoping to take him in. We weren't counting on you showing up."

"*I* wasn't counting on me showing up."

He leveled his gaze with her. "What I'm trying to figure out is why you were sent there."

Rocco twisted his head as he waited for his words to settle in her mind.

A moment later, her lips parted in realization. "You don't think my brother sent me there to put me in the middle of a bad situation, do you?"

He tilted his head again and waited for her to draw her own conclusions.

"He wouldn't do that," she insisted. "You heard him tell me over the phone. He doesn't know anything about what's going on."

"Then why did he—or his secretary—ask you to meet there at that time?" Rocco had his guys looking into both Peyton's brother and the man's secretary, Suzy. Every possibility needed to be examined right now.

"It was just a coincidence. Of course."

Rocco leaned back in his chair and folded a leg over his knee. "You and your brother have a good relationship?"

"Yes. Our parents are basically out of our lives, so we're all we both have."

"What does your brother do for a living?"

Rocco watched as Peyton swallowed hard and rubbed her throat. She was clearly uncomfortable—and for good reason. Red flags had formed a minefield.

"Anderson works in . . . finance."

Rocco didn't say anything . . . but someone who worked in finance seemed like the most likely person to be involved in something like this.

"Does he have any connections in the international business world?" Rocco continued.

Peyton shrugged, her eyes flickering back and forth in thought. "We don't really talk about his work. Finance bores me. I'm more of the creative type."

"Understood." Peyton didn't seem like the type who'd care about those details. She was probably too busy imagining new cupcake flavor combinations or ways to decorate them. There was nothing wrong with that. In fact, it suited her personality.

She shifted and pulled her legs in crisscross style. "What does all this mean for me? You've brought me here, away from everything, including my business. I have nothing with me. I don't understand what's really going on. I'm feeling . . . trapped, I suppose."

Rocco softened his voice, needing to make a few things clear with her—in the gentlest way possible. His father had been a diplomat. Rocco had been taught by the best how to soothe otherwise ragged situations.

"We're not holding you captive if that's what you're implying," he began. "But you're probably not going to be safe at your apartment or with your friends. As we talked about earlier, now that these guys have seen your face, even if you weren't a target before, you're most likely a target now."

Her face paled. "So I just stay here . . . indefinitely?"

"No, that's not what I'm saying. But we need to figure out how to handle the situation. As soon as you're safe, you can resume life as normal."

"Wait." She pointed at herself. "I'm a *situation* now?"

"Don't take that the wrong way. We just need to figure out—"

"I can't believe this is happening." Peyton swung her head back and forth before lowering her face into her hands.

Reality was clearly hitting her—and hitting her like a ton of bricks at that.

Rocco scooted closer and rested a hand on her back. He needed to keep her grounded—and to let her know she wasn't alone.

Maybe digging into the details would help her now.

"There are two things at play." He kept his voice low as he started. "The first is that we don't want you to get hurt. The second is if we can figure out why you were tricked into showing up at the scene tonight, we'll likely figure out who else is involved."

Peyton sucked in a deep breath and seemed to pull herself together a moment. "Of course, I can help. Whatever you need. I just want to get back to my life. I have employees to pay. I have to pay rent on that storefront. My front window is broken, and anyone could go in right now and steal my equipment. I know this may seem like a routine job for you—just a blip in your workload—but for me, this is my life. This is what I worked hard to save all my money for. That bakery is the manifestation of . . . of my dreams."

Rocco's heart pounded into his chest when he heard the passion in her voice.

"We're going to do everything we can to get you back there and to protect your business. Just be patient with us as we try to sort through all the details. And, by the way, I had a friend go to your shop and put a board over your broken window."

Rocco had connections in Norfolk from when he was stationed in the area as a SEAL.

"Thank you. I appreciate that." Peyton stared at him a moment before finally nodding. "Okay. I'm the busiest on the weekends, and today's Tuesday, so maybe I'll be back by Saturday. Then I can pretend like none of this ever happened."

And skip on her merry way, clicking her heels behind her as flowers bloom and birds sing.

That was Rocco's impression after talking to Peyton.

She was definitely a glass-half-full type, the "if life hands you lemons, make lemon cupcakes" poster child.

If Peyton could pretend none of this ever

happened, then this woman was much stronger than he was.

And, if that was the case, Rocco had to admit he was a little envious.

PEYTON LAY IN BED, even though she knew sleep was a distant reality.

She wanted to be in her own home, in her own bed, with her favorite pillow tucked beneath her head.

Instead, she was in this strange place.

She'd drawn the shades, trying to block the sunlight, but the brightness crept in anyway. It reminded her of a lesson they'd talked about in Bible study.

A light in a dark room always dispelled the dark. But there was no such thing as darkness in the light.

Did that apply to her situation right now? She wasn't sure. But she tucked that nugget of wisdom into the back of her mind.

She should be heading to her bakery right now preparing for the morning rush. She'd had plans of making caramel delight, cookies and cream, and even root beer flavored cupcakes.

But that wouldn't be happening today.

Would it ever happen again?

Peyton couldn't think like that. Of *course* it would. First, she just needed to get past this . . . this . . . this *situation* as Rocco had called it.

Finally, after several minutes of tossing and turning, Peyton sat up in bed.

So this Rocco guy seemed pretty on top of things. He seemed trustworthy. But what if he wasn't?

The thought made her heart pound harder.

Peyton had always been too trusting. That trait had been her downfall on more than one occasion. What if she was doing that same thing right now?

After all, she'd trusted Rodger, and he'd been the biggest mistake of her life.

Her cheeks heated at the memory. She'd been so stupid to fall for him. But he'd been everything she wasn't, and she was drawn to him for that reason.

Never again.

Peyton needed to let *somebody* know where she was. If these guys were the trained, deadly operatives they claimed to be, they could make her disappear and no one would ever know what happened to her.

Beads of sweat sprinkled across her forehead—but not like toppings on a cupcake. More like land bombs in a field before total destruction occurred.

Was she overthinking this? Peyton wasn't sure. But she *did* know she'd lived a relatively naïve, sheltered life.

Her brother often reminded her that her heart was too wide open, that she needed to be more guarded.

The last time Peyton had decided to throw caution to the wind, she'd ended up dating Rodger.

With those thoughts in mind, Peyton grabbed her phone. Quickly, she dialed her best friend's number.

The two of them had been friends since high school. While other people had gotten married, she and Karen were still single. They liked to do everything together. Movie nights. Shopping. Vacations.

Karen had also helped Peyton realize she needed to break up with Rodger. She had gone out on a limb for her, and Peyton would be forever grateful for that. Karen had helped Peyton realize just how often Rodger talked down to her and lacked respect. No one else had said anything to her. Only Karen—until after they'd broken up.

Peyton held her breath as she waited for her friend to answer. Talking to Karen always made her feel better.

But the phone rang and rang until finally going to voicemail.

Peyton ended the call and stared at her screen.

That was weird. Her friend *always* answered.

So why wasn't she answering now?

Peyton groaned. Maybe Karen was in the middle of something like checking out at the grocery store. Maybe she would return the call soon.

Until then, Peyton would wait.

Because she needed to get her racing thoughts under control, and talking to a friend was the only way she knew to do that.

CHAPTER NINE

ROCCO SAT AT HIS COMPUTER, staring at the notes he'd taken about everything that had happened in the past eleven hours.

His guys had looked into the backgrounds of Anderson Ellison as well as Suzy Belmont. Both had squeaky-clean records and no apparent connection to Tartus Enterprises. Rocco had also listened to the voicemail Suzy had sent Peyton. The recording sounded legit.

Now he was going to look into Peyton Ellison.

There was a reason she'd shown up at the scene last night—that she'd been lured there, to be more precise. He needed to figure out what that reason was.

How was that woman connected with someone

potentially selling company secrets? Or, if she wasn't directly connected, why had somebody wanted to involve her? Who was that person?

Rocco typed her name into the search engine, unsure what kind of results would pop up online.

More hits filled his screen than he'd expected.

Rocco quickly scanned several articles before clicking on the one that looked the most promising.

He read the text before letting out a grunt.

Apparently, once a week, Peyton delivered cupcakes to the homeless all over Norfolk. She said she'd started baking cupcakes because they help make the world a better place, and if she could cheer up just one person, that was all that mattered.

Several other articles indicated the same type of charitable spirit. Peyton had always been quick to donate her baked goods to fundraisers and other causes, saying that making the world brighter day by day was just something small she could do.

If sunshine could be bottled, that bottle would be named Peyton Ellison.

Rocco wished he could say he understood that kind of pure joy. He wished he had the luxury of wearing rose-colored glasses.

But he didn't. He had seen too much. Been through too much. Lost too much.

His gut lurched at the memories.

He pushed the thoughts aside and continued to scroll. This was no time to relive past events. Not with so much on the line in the present.

But nothing he found indicated why somebody might target Peyton.

Rocco sat back and rubbed the skin between his eyes.

He tried to make sense of the situation, but he needed more information first.

Who were Peyton's parents? Did they have some type of affiliation with Branson's company? Could one of Peyton's employees be using her cupcake business as a front for something else?

Those were the questions Rocco needed answered.

His head pounded harder, and he drew in a deep breath, trying to keep it under control.

He heard a beep and opened his eyes. A breaking news story appeared at the top of his screen.

He sucked in a breath when he read the words there.

Four Men Wanted in Late-Night Shooting in Norfolk.

He clicked on the link.

Blurry images appeared.

Images of Rocco and his guys.

Most people wouldn't be able to make their features out. But still . . .

Where had these images even come from?

Rocco and his team had checked the area for security cameras and had found none.

He shook his head. Something didn't make sense.

And now that video put even more pressure on them. No doubt the police would be looking for them soon.

That meant they were living on borrowed time.

As someone knocked on his door, he looked up and saw Chloe Henderson standing there. She was one of the administrative assistants for Blackout.

"Mr. Foster, you have someone here to see you."

"Who is that?" Were the police already here?

"Ms. Peyton Ellison. She's in the lobby waiting for you."

He released his breath. So much for her getting some rest.

Rocco rose.

But maybe that was okay.

Because they didn't have any time to waste.

He'd tell Colton about the news report.

Then he needed to get to know Peyton better so he could discover some answers.

PEYTON PACED in the lobby as she waited for Rocco to emerge. Her thoughts wouldn't stop racing.

She'd never been the type to sit around doing nothing. When she had free time, she'd always been baking. Or cleaning up after she baked—because she always made a huge mess whenever she was in the kitchen.

Peyton gave herself permission to be free—also known as messy—during the creative process. Then, when she was done, she faced the consequences and spent hours cleaning. But the payoff was always worth it. A few minutes of enjoyment followed by a few more minutes of doing the things she hated.

She looked up as somebody stepped into the lobby. When she saw Rocco striding toward her, her heart pounded into her chest again and her cheeks heated.

She really wished her body would stop reacting like that.

The last time she'd fallen for a guy who was all macho and tough, it hadn't ended well. Macho, tough guys had a tendency to want to control Peyton. They saw her happy-go-lucky attitude and assumed that she was weak.

But she wasn't. In fact, she was getting stronger all the time. People could underestimate her all they wanted. She liked seeing the shock on their faces when she proved them wrong.

"I thought you'd be sleeping." Rocco paused in front of her and stuffed his hands into the pockets of his black slacks.

Why did he always seem so suave and easygoing? Those very qualities rattled her.

"I can't sleep." Peyton pushed a wayward curl behind her ear. "I tried to call my friend, the one I mentioned possibly staying with earlier. Karen. I figured somebody would need to know where I was. But she's not answering."

He shrugged. "Maybe she's busy."

"I tried to text her too, and I haven't heard back. It's not like her. It's been an hour, and I've still heard nothing."

"Are you sure you're not overreacting? That the situation hasn't heightened your emotions?"

Great, maybe Rocco *wasn't* different. Maybe he was just like everybody else—always brushing off her instincts.

Peyton narrowed her gaze, not backing down. "I'm telling you, this isn't like her."

Rocco stared at her another moment before decision filled his gaze and he nodded. "Then let's see what we can find out for you."

Relief rushed through her. Her defenses had risen as she'd prepared herself to fight for what she knew was the truth. Thankfully, she hadn't had to.

Rocco could be reasonable.

She thanked God for that.

She followed Rocco down the hall and back into his office. He took a seat behind a desk and pulled up a chair beside him so Peyton could see his computer screen.

As Peyton sat beside him, their arms brushed.

She drew in a quick breath as electricity shot through her.

No, not electricity. *Gratitude*. She couldn't read too much into her reactions.

She'd have to keep reminding herself of that fact.

"Tell me your friend's name again." Rocco was clearly unaffected by their accidental touch—as he should be.

"Her name is Karen Martin. She lives in Norfolk. I can give you her address if you want."

"Let's start with her name and see what we can

find out for you. She must be really important to you."

"She's my best friend. She's been there for me when nobody else has."

He offered a quick smile. "It's nice to have people like that in our lives, isn't it?"

"It is." Peyton leaned back, again surprised at how laid-back Rocco was. She'd expected to hear cynicism in his voice. But there had been none.

As he typed in a few things on his computer, she glanced around his office. There were pictures of him in what appeared to be the Middle East. In full military gear.

But not all of them were of him about to go into combat.

There were also pictures of him with children outside villages.

Pictures of him with groups of locals in what appeared to be small communities in Afghanistan or Iraq.

Then there were pictures of him dressed to the nines and standing beside a regal-looking man with an American flag behind him.

Just what was this guy's story? Her curiosity grew.

Before she could ask, Peyton sensed a change in

the air around her. She glanced at the computer screen that Rocco stared at.

And as she did, her eyes widened.

A news article filled the screen.

A picture of Karen stretched below the headline.

Her friend had been killed in a drive-by shooting last night, right outside her apartment.

A cry escaped from Peyton as tears blurred her vision.

All this had happened, and now Karen?

Was her friend really dead?

This nightmare kept getting worse and worse.

CHAPTER TEN

COMPASSION PANGED in Rocco's chest when he saw the grief spread across Peyton's face. "I'm so sorry."

Peyton shook her head and opened her mouth, but no words came out. She only stared at the computer screen, at the picture of her friend with her honey-blonde hair, bright smile, and purple glasses.

He grabbed a tissue box and handed her one. She dabbed her eyes. But instead of falling to pieces, she almost seemed frozen with shock.

"I can't believe this." Her voice sounded scratchy. "It can't be a coincidence, can it?"

Rocco wished he had something different to tell her. "It doesn't appear likely."

"What now? What do we do? Is this my fault?" As soon as Peyton asked that last question, her voice broke and more tears flowed.

Rocco placed a hand on her back, hating the fact she was alone right now. Well, she wasn't alone. She had him. But Rocco was a stranger, and he didn't want to overstep. The woman was clearly still wary of him—as she should be.

"This isn't your fault, Peyton," he murmured. "We don't know what's going on. But we're all working to get to the bottom of it."

She raised her head just enough to lean her forehead into the palm of her hand as her arm rested on his desk. Based on her body language, that was all that was holding her up right now.

"So, what now?" she asked. "Do I call the police? Do I give a statement? What about Karen's family? I should be the one who tells them."

Rocco frowned. "If this article has already been posted, then her family already knows. The police get in touch with family before announcing names to the press in cases like this."

Peyton shook her head. "They must be feeling so awful right now. I wish I could help them."

Rocco had a feeling that Peyton would bring them cupcakes if she were there. And somehow, cupcakes would make a very grim situation just a touch brighter.

Maybe she was onto something.

"Can I call them?" she asked.

"If that would make you feel better. In the meantime, I'll call the authorities and see if there's anything they need from you." Even as he said the words, he knew how tricky that would be. Talking to the police could mean they'd arrest him.

She looked up at him, her eyes still brimming with tears. "I just don't want to sit here and not do anything."

"I was hoping you'd say that. Because we're going to need your help in order to get to the bottom of things here."

Peyton sniffed loudly again before adamantly nodding. "I'll do whatever you want. We need to find whoever did this."

"Okay then. Why don't we go get you something to eat? Maybe some more coffee. Or if you need some time alone, that's okay too."

"I'll take a coffee. Then I want to help you. Whoever did this can't get away with it."

Rocco nodded again, hoping Peyton would be able to hold up through this. Because digging into the possibilities of what was going on wouldn't be easy.

But he would be right there beside Peyton for whatever she needed.

PEYTON LET OUT A SIGH, trying to hold back her frustration as she sat across from Rocco in his office.

At least looking into her past would distract her from thinking about Karen and the horrible ordeal she must have gone through. If she let herself, she could too easily imagine the pain and fear her friend had endured.

Poor Karen.

Peyton shook her head. There would be time to think about that later. Right now, she would concentrate on putting an end to this horrible situation.

She turned to Rocco. "I'm sorry. I know you're trying to figure something out. But my family was normal. I have no idea why somebody would target me. All I do is make cupcakes and pastries."

"You're right—that's no reason for you to be a target."

When Rocco said things with that British accent, everything seemed so much classier somehow.

Peyton wanted to make some Earl Grey cupcakes and eat crumpets with her pinky raised.

Peyton let out a sigh as her thoughts turned serious. How could she even think something like that at a time like this? Guilt assaulted her.

"Is it strange that I *want* there to be something in my family's background?" she finally asked. "I need an explanation. I want things to make sense. But they don't."

Rocco leaned back in his chair and nodded. "I know what you're saying. And I'm sorry."

"So what now?" Peyton looked up at Rocco, hoping he held all the answers.

But she knew that was impossible. Nobody had all the answers. It seemed like everybody was just doing their best to get through things. Peyton understood that. She'd been there before. She was there now. And she'd certainly be there again in the future.

Rocco pushed to his feet and released the air from his lungs. "Now, I think we need to take a breather. Do you feel up to a walk?"

"I'm allowed to leave this building?"

He tilted his head as if softening. "I mean it when I say you're here by your own free will. You're not our prisoner. You haven't hired us to keep you safe.

You're here simply because you're in a bad situation and you needed a place to go."

Something about his words made Peyton feel better. Because there were moments she *did* feel like she was being held captive.

"A walk sounds great. For sure, being outside can work wonders at times."

"Very well then." Rocco rose, all six plus feet of him.

He reached for her hand to help her up. Peyton practically felt like a child next to him. Something about the man made her feel safe, and it wasn't just his size. Protectiveness seemed to ooze from him.

A few minutes later, he lightly touched her back as he accompanied her outside. Even though they'd arrived here when the sun had been coming up, Peyton hadn't gotten a good look at this place. But now that she had . . . she almost felt like she was at a private resort. A private military resort.

A main building stood at the center of the property, almost reminding her of a beachside hotel. Two wings stretched from the main lobby. Dormers had been built onto the roof, gray siding covered the walls, and a large porch welcomed people as they arrived.

In the distance, she saw an obstacle-training

course, much like those she might see at a boot camp. She thought she'd also seen a shooting range and a couple of other buildings. A fence with razor wire across the top outlined the entire property as far as Peyton could see.

The two of them started down a sandy trail toward the water.

"As I started to tell you earlier, that's the Pamlico Sound, one of the largest estuaries here on the East Coast, right after the Chesapeake Bay," Rocco explained.

"It's beautiful. So peaceful."

"I think so too."

They strolled along beside each other, not moving too quickly. The sunshine felt warm, the breeze balmy, and the scent of the ocean salty.

But Peyton didn't miss the fact that Rocco continued to glance around as they walked, almost as if to double-check that everything was okay.

"So what is this place exactly?" she asked. "You mentioned you worked for an organization called Blackout, but this is far more than I ever imagined."

"This is the Blackout headquarters," Rocco said. "We're a private security agency made up of former Navy SEALs."

"I didn't think the British could be a Navy SEAL."

Rocco smiled. "I get that comment a lot. My father is American, and my mother is British. I split my time between the two countries and hold a dual citizenship. It actually worked out well when I became a SEAL. My accent and knowledge of Europe came in handy a few times."

"I can imagine. What about that building back there?" Peyton nodded toward the main facility at the center of the property. "I saw a sign saying it was the Daniel Oliver Building? Who was he?"

Rocco's expression sobered. "He's a SEAL who gave his life to save all of us. His widow eventually married Colton Locke, our fearless leader. But he sacrificed everything in order to save the people he cared about. It only seemed fitting to name the building after him."

"It sounds like it." They took a few more steps when Peyton decided to change the subject. "So, tell me about Lantern Beach."

"Lantern Beach is right below Ocracoke and above Emerald Isle. You can only get here by boat or helicopter. There are no bridges."

Peyton shivered. "So it's remote."

"Yes, it is. It makes it more difficult to leave for various operations. But it also makes it a great place to get away—or to take people who need to stay safe."

Peyton glanced at Rocco. He wore black slacks and a button-up gray shirt. His hair looked neat, and there were no hints that he hadn't gotten any sleep probably in twenty-four hours. The fact that he was so attractive only made this more nerve-wracking for her.

In the meantime, she knew she looked like a wreck. Salty, humid air usually made her hair frizz. She was wearing clothes that didn't quite fit her right. She had no makeup with her.

A definite wreck.

She turned her attention back to the island—something far safer to think about. "So every time you leave here, you have to take a boat?"

"Right now, yes. But we're in the process of putting in an airstrip. We also just received a donation so we can purchase a helicopter. That will help us out greatly."

"You guys are hard core."

"We've been very blessed. We were given grants and donations to do all this. The organization has grown quickly, and no one's complaining. I'm one of the new guys here—along with the rest of the guys you met last night."

"So they sent the newbies out for that operation?"

Rocco smiled again. "Something like that."

Peyton paused beside the water and looked out over it, drawing in a deep breath. "So how do you like it here? And your new job?"

His hands remained in his pockets as he stared out over the water also. "I can't complain. It was time for me to get out of the military. After doing so many missions like I did, your body starts to break down. That kind of work begins to wreak havoc on your mental health, and it can definitely be hard on all your relationships. I knew it was time."

"Did the rest of the guys on your team leave when you did?"

"Actually, we didn't all get out at the same time. Axel has been out for two years. He hurt his knee and couldn't go back on the field. Beckett is the most recent to end his term. He had family issues he needed to deal with. And Gabe left . . . well, Gabe left because he's a team player if I've ever seen one, and he wanted to stick with us."

Silence stretched between them for a few minutes.

"I still can't believe I'm here." Peyton stared out over the water, realizing she couldn't even see land on the other side. It almost looked like a gentle ocean of its own. "All this feels surreal."

"I'm sure it does. But we're going to find you some answers. When we're certain you're safe, I'll have no qualms about you leaving here. I just don't want to see you go back home only to get hurt."

Something about the starkness of his words caused a panicked flutter to fill Peyton's chest.

This was a nightmare. Yet it was also her new reality.

She had to figure out how she was going to deal with it.

CHAPTER ELEVEN

"I NEED TO TALK TO YOU." Beckett found Rocco as soon as he and Peyton stepped back inside the Daniel Oliver Building. Urgency etched each of his friend's actions, his expression.

"Is it about my friend, Karen?" Peyton rushed, worry filling her voice.

Beckett glanced at her and shook his head. "No, I'm sorry. It's about a different matter."

Rocco turned to Peyton, hating to cut their time short. But she wasn't here for a social visit, no matter how entertaining and endearing the woman might be.

"If you don't mind, I need a moment," he murmured.

"I think I might go lie down for just a few

minutes." She pointed with her thumb to the stairway. "That will give you some time to sort things out too."

"When you're ready, come back downstairs. You can talk to Chloe, and she'll come get me. Or this is my cell phone number." Rocco handed her a card.

Peyton shoved it into her pocket, muttered thank you, and then headed back to the stairway leading to the second floor.

When she was gone, Rocco turned to Beckett, anxious to hear what was so urgent. "What's going on?"

"Frank at the front gate just called," Beckett said. "He was reviewing some security footage, and he thought he saw some strange movements in the woods around our facilities. He couldn't make out much in the videos, but he wanted to alert us in case we wanted to check it out."

"Absolutely. Did you see the footage also?"

"I did. It almost looked like there was someone out there. But the images were hard to make out."

They stepped outside and headed toward the gate.

"You think that whoever opened fire last night knows who we are?" Beckett asked. "Where we are?"

Rocco frowned. "I think it's a possibility. Based

on everything that's happened so far, these people have always been one step ahead of us."

"I don't like the sound of that."

"I don't either."

They reached the gate and were buzzed through to the other side. They made their way down the edge of the woods that ran along the south side of the Blackout complex. As they walked, they searched the trees and ground, looking for anything that might have been left behind by somebody.

Rocco's best guess was a camera—a way of spying on them.

But he bristled when he saw a device in the tree.

That was a gun.

Why had someone mounted a rifle in the tree?

At once, he knew.

He grabbed Beckett's arm.

"Run!"

Just as they dove for cover, bullets filled the air.

BEFORE PEYTON TRIED to get some rest, she looked at her phone again. She only had 20 percent left on her battery. Hopefully, someone here had a charger she could borrow.

Even though she was beginning to feel exhausted from everything that had happened, she knew her brother should be back from Michigan by now.

She wanted to talk to him. She wanted his feedback. Needed to tell him about Karen.

Peyton dialed his number and prayed he'd answer.

He picked up on the first ring, and worry stretched through his voice. "Peyton? Is that you? Are you okay?"

"I'm fine." She kept her voice level as she tried to reassure him. "Are you home?"

"No, my flight got delayed. I probably won't be able to come back until tomorrow now. They've been having a lot of storms, and a ton of flights are grounded."

"I'm sorry to hear that." She paused, not wanting to voice her next question aloud. But she had no choice. "Did you hear about Karen?"

"What about her?"

Peyton licked her lips, wishing she didn't have to say the words. But Anderson needed to know. "Anderson . . . Karen was killed last night. In a drive-by shooting."

"What?" Surprise laced Anderson's voice. "Peyton . . . I had no idea."

"It's been a shock, to say the least."

"Have you gone to visit her family? Are they okay?"

She drew her knees to her chest, wondering how her life had gotten to this point. "No, I'm not in Virginia anymore."

"What? Where are you then?" The questions continued to pour from him.

Peyton explained what had happened, thankful to have some privacy so she could speak freely. She felt like she'd been under the microscope ever since those guys rescued her. Though she understood their reasoning, the pressure she felt made her neck muscles kink with stress.

"I don't like the sound of that, Peyton." Concern filled Anderson's voice.

"What do you mean? I'm safe here. Safer than I would be up in Virginia by myself—especially after what happened to Karen." Was she trying to convince herself or Anderson? Peyton wasn't sure.

"But you don't know anything about these guys. How do you even know they are who they claim to be?"

"They're former military. Why shouldn't I trust them?"

"Because you know nothing about them other than what they told you."

She frowned and nibbled on her bottom lip. "My gut tells me they're okay."

"But your gut isn't always right. I hate to remind you of that."

Peyton bit down, grinding her teeth like she always did when she was stressed. The last thing she wanted right now was to have to defend herself. Yet she couldn't let that comment pass either.

"We've all made mistakes before," she reminded him.

"I know. But you're my little sis. I want to look out for you."

That was right. His intentions were good. It was his approach that needed refining. "I appreciate that. But I feel safe here."

Anderson stayed quiet a moment until finally saying, "Okay then. I'll call you when I get back. Then you can come and stay with me. There's no need for you to be with strangers. I would be there with you right now if I could."

"Thanks." But Peyton wasn't quite ready to get off

the phone yet. She still had more on her mind. "You don't know anything about what happened, do you?"

"You mean, about the incident last night? I have no idea. I'm still trying to figure out why someone would use my name to get you out to that location. It doesn't make any sense to me. I couldn't sleep all night last night thinking about it."

"Same here." She frowned. "Listen, if you discover anything, let me know."

"I will. Stay safe, Sis. I love you."

"I love you too." Peyton ended the call and held her phone to her chest.

Was her brother right? Was she being too trusting again?

But when she remembered her conversation with Rocco earlier, she'd felt so at ease. So comfortable with the man.

She remembered the photos she'd seen of him. Photos of him helping people overseas.

What was there not to trust about that?

Peyton didn't know.

But she'd probably be wise to remain on guard.

CHAPTER TWELVE

ROCCO PUSHED himself behind a tree as more gunfire filled the air.

He held his breath as he glanced at Beckett, who was also behind a tree.

Eventually, the gun would run out of ammo.

Until then, they needed to stay put.

Finally, it stopped.

Rocco motioned for Beckett to remain still another moment. They needed to make sure there were no more motion-activated weapons around.

Nothing happened—except for the yells he heard in the distance.

The guys from Blackout had obviously heard the shots and were on their way.

"You okay?" he asked Beckett.

"That was some crazy stuff."

"You can say that again," Rocco muttered.

Cautiously, they stepped out.

The area looked clear, but they'd still need to watch their steps.

"What just happened?" Colton and Axel ran up.

Rocco pointed to the gun in the trees. "That happened. Must have been motion-activated."

"Beckett, you check it out for us," Colton said.

Out of everyone in the group, Beckett was their weapons expert.

"I'll check the area for more guns," Colton added.

It appeared they had even more work to do here.

AN HOUR LATER, they all met back in the conference room.

"Play us that voicemail again," Colton said. "The one Suzy Belmont left Peyton. I want to hear it."

Rocco had sent the recording to his phone. He found it and hit Play. Everyone leaned close as the woman's voice filled the air.

"Hey, Peyton. It's Suzy. Anderson's in the middle of something right now, but he wanted me to call you and ask you to bring two dozen of your best-ever cupcakes to a party this evening. He said there will be a lot of influencers there who could help create some buzz about your new business. But there's a catch. The party is late, and it's in the warehouse district. Anderson said he'll meet you outside the building and walk you in. Unless I hear otherwise, we'll see you then. Have a great night, Pey!"

Rocco glanced at everyone as the recording ended, waiting for their reactions.

Colton frowned. "Did you check the number?"

"I did," Rocco said. "It's Suzy's work phone number."

"Did you try to call Suzy?" Beckett narrowed his eyes, his always-serious face as intense as ever.

"I did," Rocco said. "She didn't answer. Someone else at Anderson's office picked up and said Suzy called out sick today."

Colton grunted. "Peculiar timing."

"I agree," Rocco said. "So where does this leave us? Did Suzy set Peyton up?"

"You said Peyton is clean, right?" Axel flipped his pen in the air.

"No record," Rocco confirmed. "No parking tickets even."

Colton shifted back in his seat and let out a long

breath. "Let's say someone else sent Peyton out there. Maybe they forced Suzy to leave that message under duress. We'll figure that part out later. Right now, we need to figure out why. *Why* did someone target Peyton?"

Rocco had asked himself that question many times already. "I can't figure it out. She's involved in the community, owns her own business, and seems like sunshine in a bottle."

"Sunshine in a bottle?" Axel smirked at his description. "Interesting wording."

Rocco shrugged, learning long ago not to let his guys get under his skin. "You've met her. You can't deny it."

"It's true. I can't." Axel smirked again. "But that doesn't help us, does it?"

Rocco sighed. "No, it doesn't."

"She wasn't chosen randomly." Colton's jaw stiffened. "Someone wanted her there."

"But who?" Gabe asked. "Who would want to interrupt the exchange? Not the person selling the info. Not the person buying the info. Not Branson. So who does that leave?"

His questions hung in the air.

Gabe was right.

The motives just weren't making sense.

The sooner they could change that... the sooner they could have some sushi.

JUST AS PEYTON drifted to sleep, "If You're Happy and You Know It" began blaring. Her head popped up, and she grabbed her phone from beside her pillow. Her heart raced at the jarring song. It had seemed like a great ring tone at the time she chose it.

Mentally, Peyton had been transported back in time to that warehouse again. She'd had those cupcakes in her hands. The stranger had knocked them to the ground. Then Rocco had tackled her. Then the gunfire had erupted.

Thankfully, right now Peyton was safe.

She glanced at the screen and saw her brother's name. Why was he calling her back now? How much time had passed since they last talked?

She glanced at the clock.

It was nearly four o'clock. She really had been sleeping, hadn't she? More deeply than she'd thought.

Peyton quickly put the phone to her ear. "Anderson? What's going on? Are you okay?"

"I'm fine. But since my flight was delayed, I decided to do some research."

The brisk tone of his voice made her feel uneasy. "And?"

"Look, Peyton, I don't want to alarm you. But I looked into this Blackout organization, and I'm not sure they're the people you want to be with."

"What do you mean?" Peyton's spine stiffened as she waited to hear where he was going with this. What had he discovered?

"These guys all got out of the military prematurely. They faced traumatic situations while they were overseas. Now they're private security experts? Who's to say that they're not the ones behind everything that's happened? People like that . . . while I admire their sacrifice, their experiences can mess with their mental state."

Certainly, she hadn't heard him correctly. He was making a big leap with that conclusion. "That doesn't make sense, Anderson. One of these guys pushed me out of the way before I got shot. He saved my life."

Her cheeks heated as she remembered feeling Rocco's protective arms around her as gunshots rang out.

"What if it was all staged? What if they did that to earn your trust?"

His words felt like a bomb had swept through the room. Her head throbbed as she tried to even find a response to that. "Why would they do that?"

"Look, I'm just trying to think all this through. Someone sent you a voicemail to get you to that location. Then someone opened fire. These guys rescued you, and now you're basically at their mercy. They earned your trust . . . maybe so they could get whatever information they need from you."

Her brother wasn't making any sense. His theory was outlandish . . . then again, so was this entire situation.

But there was one thing Anderson was forgetting.

"I don't have any information," she finally countered.

Her brother didn't miss a beat. "For some reason, these guys must think you have something to do with all this. Plus, I discovered there used to be a cult there on Lantern Beach. Who says these people didn't rebrand themselves and emerge as a private security organization? Maybe you've gotten yourself wrapped up with a group of people who are dangerous."

Peyton shook her head. "I think your reasoning is flimsy. I'm sorry. I know you're concerned, and I know you're watching out for me, but you're off base."

"There was a news story on TV about them—four men are wanted for opening fire in Norfolk last night."

"I was there. They weren't the ones firing."

Anderson sighed. "Peyton . . . I didn't want to bring this up, but I have no choice. I looked into Karen's death. I called a couple of people back in Norfolk. It turns out, she was killed about two hours before these guys grabbed you."

"Okay . . ." Peyton wasn't sure what he was getting at—or she didn't want to acknowledge it.

"Didn't you say they were driving a black van?"

"Yes . . ."

"And didn't they have machine guns?"

"I think that's what they were, but—"

"Peyton, who's to say these guys didn't kill Karen before coming to find you?"

Her blood froze at that thought. Peyton shook her head. "No . . . what sense would that make?"

"It turns out that Karen was going to call you and see if you guys wanted to meet up for a late dinner. If she'd done that, then you probably wouldn't have made that cupcake delivery."

Peyton sucked in a shallow breath. "How do you even know that?"

"Because I called Karen's roommate, and that's what she told me. Karen was on her way out to her car because she'd left her phone there. That's when somebody drove past and shot her."

Nausea swirled in Peyton's gut as denial pummeled her like machine-gun fire. Karen was killed before those men shot at her? What sense did that make?

She desperately wanted to connect the pieces, to know the truth.

But that task felt impossible.

"I can't believe that," she finally said.

"Listen to me, Peyton. Is there any way you can get out of there?"

She glanced around the apartment, trying to keep a level head about the situation—a level head and an open mind. Letting her fear overcome her would only be to her detriment.

"I mean, I suppose I could just walk away," she said. "They told me I'm not a prisoner here."

"They actually said that?" Incredulousness captured his voice.

"Yes, they said that I have free will to come or go. They can't be that bad if they said that, right?"

"They're just trying to butter you up, to make you feel safe and secure. Based on what you've told me, that place is locked down. There's no way they'll let you leave."

She swallowed hard, not liking the sound of that. "You really think that?"

"I do. You need to get out of there. In the meantime, I'll call the local police and let them know what's going on."

"Anderson . . ." Fear began to trickle into her tone—and any sense of peace she'd had faded.

"I have a bad feeling about this, Peyton. Get out of there. Now."

CHAPTER THIRTEEN

ROCCO and the rest of the team stood, their meeting finally wrapping up.

They'd called Branson and given him the update. As Rocco had thought, the man hadn't been happy.

But the team had ultimately decided to send Gabe undercover to work at the company and try to figure out who was attempting to sell company secrets. Branson had it narrowed down to five people he thought were most suspect—people who would more easily have access to that information.

Gabe would leave tonight so he could be there bright and early for work the next day.

The guy was sometimes too smart for his own good, but Rocco thought he'd be perfect for this assignment—especially since he knew his way around a computer better than anyone else on the team. Throw on some glasses and Gabe's vast knowledge of pour-over coffee, and he'd fit right in at the startup company.

As the rest of the guys filed out of the room, Colton called to Rocco. He held his iPad in his hands, and his forehead was wrinkled with concern.

"What's going on?" Rocco paused near him.

"I had a friend of mine check some security footage around Peyton's place of business. I wanted to see if we could catch an image of who broke her window—I figured it might lead us to some other answers as well."

"What did you find?" Rocco asked.

Colton frowned as he held out the iPad.

Rocco braced himself for what he might see.

He watched the images on the screen. The storefront looked calm and gray. The time stamp read 11:42.

That must have been right after Peyton left to deliver the cupcakes.

He held his breath as he waited.

Finally, a figure appeared at the corner of the screen. Based on the angle, the person was shadowed.

And the person was . . . a woman.

He hadn't expected that.

The woman held a brick. She glanced up and down the sidewalk before heaving the brick into the glass. The window shattered.

Then the woman smiled.

Before she left, she glanced around again.

This time, the camera caught her face.

And Peyton stared back at him.

PEYTON GLANCED AROUND THE APARTMENT, wondering what she could take with her. But she hadn't brought anything, therefore she had nothing to take along. Nothing except her wallet and her phone, which was down to five percent right now.

Should she really do this? In essence, it should be as easy as walking out the door and through the gate. There should be nothing to stop her.

But what would she do when she left? She had no car. She was alone on the island. She had hardly any money in her wallet.

Peyton supposed the most logical thing to do was go to the police station and explain everything that happened. Maybe the police could help her figure out something.

But she had no idea how far away the police station was. That wasn't to mention the fact that she'd worn flats yesterday. They weren't the best walking shoes. Then again, she hadn't planned on doing much walking.

Her brother's words echoed in her mind. *They're just trying to butter you up, to make you feel safe and secure. Based on what you've told me, that place is on lockdown. There's no way they'll let you leave.*

Was Anderson right? Was Peyton in danger by being here?

She glanced out the window. In the distance she spotted four men on the lawn running some kind of physical-training drill.

Were they preparing for something deadly? What if their intentions weren't as noble as she wanted to believe? Could her optimism ultimately end up being the death of her?

The questions left her feeling unsettled.

Going to the local police couldn't hurt anything. If these guys were on the up-and-up, the police could confirm that. If they weren't, then Peyton could get away from them.

That settled it. That was what Peyton needed to do.

Quietly, she slipped from the apartment.

She glanced up and down the hall.

There was no one.

Moving quickly, Peyton started toward the stairway.

As soon as she reached the first step, two women opened the door on the floor above and started down. Before Peyton could hide, they spotted her and offered warm smiles.

"Welcome to Blackout," a pretty brunette with short hair and a growing belly said. "I'm Elise. Maybe you met my husband, Colton?"

Peyton shook her head, not recalling meeting him. But she couldn't show how skittish she felt right now. She needed to pretend to be friendly.

"I don't think so. Not yet at least. I'm Peyton."

"I overheard the guys talking about what happened." Elise frowned. "It sounds like you've been through quite the ordeal. If you need to talk, Bethany and I are great listeners. We could grab coffee sometime and maybe offer a moment of normalcy to this crazy situation."

The woman seemed sincere and kind. So did her blonde friend, Bethany, who smiled sweetly beside her.

These two certainly didn't seem abnormal in any way.

Then again, cult members often blended in, didn't they?

No, these people weren't a part of a cult. Her brother had just been putting ideas in her head. It was ridiculous, really.

But Peyton had researched the cult, the one that had been known as Gilead's Cove. They had indeed taken up residence here on the island before they were taken down. Not all the members had been arrested—some had been innocent civilians caught up in false hope.

What if some of them had recreated themselves into a new organization?

No. She mentally shook her head. That thought was crazy.

"That sounds nice," Peyton finally said. "But right now, I was going to head downstairs for a quick snack. Do you think that's okay?"

"Of course," Bethany said. "The kitchen is stocked, so help yourself. Would you like us to show you where to go?"

"I think I should be able to find it but thank you." Peyton offered a smile, hoping it didn't show the nerves she felt.

As the women detoured onto the second floor, Peyton hurried down the steps. Her heart raced.

She hated questioning herself. She really did.

But her brother had always looked out for her. Anderson had never led her astray before. He wouldn't lead her astray now either.

She slowed her steps when she reached the lobby, reminding herself not to draw any unnecessary attention.

As she glanced around, she saw no one.

But Peyton knew at least four men were outside on the other side of the building doing drills. Still, she'd need to be cautious.

She slipped outside, the sinking sun flooding her face. When the doors closed behind her, she knew she wouldn't be able to get back inside. Not without a code or a badge.

Reluctantly, she let go of the door, realizing there was no turning back now.

She glanced around. The coast was clear, as the saying went.

Peyton remained at the edge of the building before darting toward the trees in the distance. She'd use them for cover as she ran toward the gate.

Now she just had to pray she'd be able to get past that gate.

Because there was no way she could climb the fence with the razor wire atop it.

CHAPTER FOURTEEN

ROCCO HATED to wake up Peyton. He knew the woman needed her rest. But he had a question that couldn't wait.

And it wasn't about that video footage.

As much as he wanted to ask her about it—and as much as he was still reeling in shock—he and Colton had decided it was best not to mention it yet. Instead, Rocco would get close to her. Try to figure out what was really going on. Dig for answers.

Because Peyton was clearly a great actress.

With her sweet and innocent disposition, she didn't seem like the type who could pull something like this off.

But she had.

Anger burned inside him when he thought

about her deception. But he needed to act like nothing was wrong.

For now.

He knocked at her apartment door.

There was no answer.

Was she a hard sleeper? Maybe she didn't hear him.

Rocco contemplated his options a moment. He wanted to respect the woman's privacy. But this matter was urgent.

"Are you looking for Peyton?" Elise exited the room across the hall and paused beside him.

He turned toward her. "I am."

"She went downstairs. Said she was going to the kitchen to get a snack."

The explanation seemed reasonable enough. "When was this?"

"Just a few minutes ago. You probably just missed her. She went down the main staircase."

Rocco frowned. "I came up the stairs on the opposite side. I'll go see if I can find her."

But when Rocco stepped into the kitchen, Peyton was nowhere to be seen. One of the housekeepers was putting away some dishes, but she said she hadn't seen Peyton either.

Strange.

Peyton came down to get food, yet she never made it into the kitchen.

A bad feeling climbed up his spine.

Quickly, he searched the rest of the areas Peyton would have access to without a badge.

She was nowhere to be found, and no one had seen her.

Just then his phone rang.

It was Arnold, a guard stationed at the front gate.

"What's going on?" Rocco asked.

"I thought you'd want to know that a woman just walked off the campus. I had no reason to stop her, but something felt off about it."

Concern ricocheted through Rocco. "Was she petite with curly, dark hair?"

"She sure was."

Peyton had left?

What in the world was she thinking?

Either way, Rocco had to find her.

Especially if what he had discovered was true.

AS PEYTON HEADED down the road, she marveled at how beautiful this island was. The landscape was rugged, like any good East Coast island might be.

The roads were sandy and dusty with a scattering of gravel and crushed oyster shells. The trees were small and scrappy. Instead of a lush green lawn, marsh grass and reeds rose up on the sides of the roads. Seagulls flew overhead, and the salty scent of the ocean floated around her.

If it wasn't for everything that had happened, Peyton might actually find herself enjoying this place.

But it was hard to forget the horrible events that had occurred over the past seventeen hours.

The Blackout campus was obviously located far out of the way from everything else on the island. No other houses were around. Instead, woods rose on one side of her and fields of marsh grass on the other. In the distance, she thought she saw a church steeple.

This walk to the police station was going to be farther than she thought.

Should she call 911?

Peyton checked her phone and frowned.

It was dead.

She sighed as she stuffed her phone back into the pocket of her jeans and picked up her pace. At least she'd be able to see anyone coming on a road like this. It was a long, straight stretch of practically nothing.

Peyton's thoughts went to Karen. Karen had just been out, going to grab her phone, when her life had ended. Peyton had no doubt that her friend had no idea what was coming. How could she?

Suddenly, her spine tightened. Only seconds earlier, Peyton had felt so safe. But how long would it be until somebody from Blackout realized that she was missing? Would they come after her? Hunt her down?

They had said that she was free to leave. But if her brother was right, that could just be their way of manipulating her and making her feel safe.

The questions crashed together in her head.

Peyton looked behind her but saw no one.

Still, she quickened her steps until she was almost jogging.

She still hadn't reached the church yet. The steeple didn't even appear to be getting any nearer.

Should she go there instead of the police station?

The building was closer. Maybe there was a parsonage beside it, and the pastor would be able to help her.

That plan seemed better than her original.

She kept moving until she finally saw a small

lane cutting through the marsh grass leading toward the church building.

Perfect.

As soon as Peyton was off the main road, she released the breath she'd been holding.

She felt safer here. Less exposed and visible.

Until a new sound filled her ears.

The rumble of tires.

Peyton jerked her head to look behind her. A dark-colored sedan headed slowly down the lane.

She wanted to believe the driver was just the pastor coming back from visiting someone ill.

But what if it wasn't?

Her heart pounded harder. She continued walking, quickening her steps.

What if it was someone from Blackout coming to grab her again? If that was the case, there would be no games this time. Peyton would know without a doubt that she really was their prisoner.

Or, if the guys at Blackout weren't guilty, what if it was one of the gunmen from last night? What if they knew she was here and had come to finish what they'd started?

She rubbed her neck, feeling as if something were choking her.

Fear tried to consume her.

But she couldn't let that happen.

Instead, she burst into a run.

The lengthy lane stretched in front of her. She still had a long way to go before she reached the church building.

But she couldn't give up.

As Peyton glanced behind her again, she saw the car had also sped up.

Her heart pounded harder.

What was she going to do?

She had nowhere to go.

Marsh grass rose on either side of the road.

Marsh grass . . . it wasn't ideal. But it was something. That car couldn't drive through the wetlands without getting stuck in the soft earth.

As the car sped closer, Peyton made a split-second decision.

She darted into the marsh.

Her feet sank into the wet, fragile ground.

But she didn't care.

All Peyton cared about was getting away . . . and staying alive.

CHAPTER FIFTEEN

JUST AS ROCCO jumped in his SUV, Axel wandered from the building. Rocco called him over, waited for Axel to climb inside, and then he took off down the road. He quickly explained to his friend what was going on.

"You're really worried about this woman . . ." Axel raised his eyebrows.

Rocco's grip tightened on the steering wheel. "I don't think she has any idea what she's gotten into."

"Do you think those guys with the machine guns know that she's here?"

His jaw clenched at the thought. "I wouldn't put it past them. It wouldn't take much for them to realize that a private security firm had been hired.

Whoever is behind this could narrow it down to us fairly easily."

"Do you think they want to kill her?"

Heat spread through Rocco's veins at the thought—the fiery kind of heat that he only felt when anger pumped through his veins.

"That's my best guess."

"There aren't that many places she could go down here."

"I can't argue with that. But we don't have any time to waste."

Rocco wondered what had gotten into Peyton. She was doing so well when he talked to her last. She'd calmed down. Acted as if she understood.

So what had changed? What triggered her to leave?

He'd worry about that later.

Right now, he just wanted to find her.

Rocco slowed as he reached the lane leading to the church.

As he glanced toward the steepled white building in the distance, he saw a dark sedan parked farther down the stretch of gravel. The driver's door was open.

But there was no sign of anybody—not Peyton or the person who'd been inside.

But his pulse thrummed in his ears like drums before a war.

Quickly, Rocco turned down the road. He'd been to this church twice since he'd arrived a couple of weeks ago, and he knew the pastor most definitely did not drive a Lexus.

Thankfully, Rocco had his gun with him.

Because, if his gut feeling was correct, he might need it.

PEYTON REMAINED LOW, trying to stay out of sight.

The man had climbed from his car. He chased her. Just as she feared.

She had to get away.

The marsh was harder to run through than she'd anticipated. The ground practically swallowed her with every step. She didn't want to even think about what kind of creatures she might encounter between these reeds.

She glanced around again. A few trees rose from the wetlands.

If Peyton could reach one of them, maybe it would offer her shelter.

As she heard reeds breaking behind her, she looked back.

Her heart rate quickened.

The man with a gun dashed through the area, trying to reach her.

But he wasn't shooting.

Not yet.

She had to keep going. Peyton didn't know where she was headed. She only knew she needed to put as much space as possible between herself and this man.

A branch caught her foot. She lunged forward. As she did, a sharp pain shot through her ankle.

Oh no. Not now.

Please, don't let it be broken.

Peyton dragged herself back to her feet. More pain shot through her ankle.

But the throbbing wasn't unbearable.

Maybe it wasn't broken, only sprained.

She had to keep moving.

Her life depended on it.

She looked up again.

One of the trees wasn't far away—maybe ten feet. If she could just make it there and lean against it for a minute.

She stumbled forward, hobbling through the marsh.

Reeds continued to snap behind her.

But the gunman remained silent.

Only silently chased her.

A shiver of fear ran down her spine.

Finally, she reached the tree, crossed behind it, and leaned into its sturdy trunk.

She tried to catch her breath.

But she didn't know where to go next or how to get somewhere safe.

Did that mean she had no chance of surviving this?

Peyton wasn't sure.

And that thought terrified her.

ROCCO SEARCHED the marsh for Peyton.

Was that where she'd gone? It was the only place that made sense—especially since that car was still here.

As he scanned the reeds, he saw nothing.

No movement.

He heard nothing.

No branches snapping.

He paused a moment, waiting for a signal as to anything hiding around him.

"What do you think?" Axel asked quietly beside him.

Rocco put a finger over his lips, motioning him to remain silent another moment.

A whimper rose from the silence.

Rocco's gaze shot in the direction of the noise.

That sound was human. He was certain of it.

A second later, Peyton's head peeked above the marsh grass. She remained hunched, as if trying to hide. Then she started forward, her steps uneven.

Was she hurt?

Was someone chasing her?

And, if so, where was this person right now?

Rocco didn't see anybody else out there.

Unless somebody else was using the reeds for cover.

And possibly waiting to attack.

Carefully, Rocco motioned for Axel to start through the marsh.

They moved slowly in case somebody was out here.

He watched as Peyton continued along, finally stopping near a gnarled live oak.

He wasn't sure how safe she'd be behind the thin branches.

When they got halfway between the road and the tree, a rustling sounded behind him.

A shot filled the air.

He and Axel ducked into the brush.

Someone was shooting at them.

But where had the shooter come from?

As if to answer the question, an engine started in the distance.

Rocco lifted his head in time to see the Lexus backing down the lane at full speed.

Toward Rocco's car.

Rocco held his breath, waiting to see if the driver would ram his vehicle.

Expertly, the man drove through the marsh, around Rocco's SUV, and finally reached the other lane. The driver squealed away.

Rocco knew he couldn't catch him.

It didn't matter. He needed to make sure Peyton was okay.

Had she been shot?

Was that why she'd been limping?

Concern ricocheted through him.

He needed to find her.

Now.

CHAPTER SIXTEEN

WHEN PEYTON HEARD THE GUNSHOT, her pulse began beating in double-time.

She sank lower into the reeds.

Her fingers still dug into the rough bark of the tree.

And she waited.

She was going to die out here, wasn't she? It would be her own fault.

Who had that man in the car been? What did he want from her?

A new sound filled the air. Tires moving across gravel.

She peered around the tree in time to see the car that had followed her leaving.

But another vehicle was parked behind it.

Were there *two* people out here hunting her?

She watched as the other driver maneuvered around the SUV at the end of the lane before speeding away.

Her heart still pounded in her chest as danger hovered in the air.

"Peyton?" someone called.

Was that . . . ?

She peered around the tree long enough to see . . . Rocco rushing toward her.

Relief filled her. But she quickly scolded herself. She shouldn't feel relieved to see Rocco.

She knew nothing about this man or his intentions or his company. If anything at this point, she should feel just as cautious around him as she felt around any stranger.

But she couldn't get away from him now. She couldn't run.

He quickly reached her and grasped her arm as he knelt beside her. "Are you okay?"

She started to nod and shift her weight. But as she did, more pain shot through her ankle.

She winced before admitting, "I think I sprained my ankle."

"I can take a look at it. But why don't we get you back to the campus first?"

Peyton wasn't sure that was where she wanted to go. She had so many questions. Too many for her comfort.

"You're still not sure if you can trust me, are you?" Rocco seemed to read her thoughts.

She shrugged, for some reason hesitant to admit it. He'd shown nothing but kindness. But what if he'd been deceiving her?

"Let me get you back to the car, check out your ankle, and then take you down to the police station," Rocco finally said. "You can tell the police chief what just happened and ask her any questions you want. How does that sound?"

It actually seemed like a great compromise.

Peyton nodded. "Okay. It's a plan."

She limped forward, trying not to show her discomfort. But it was hard to hide.

"Let me help you." Rocco turned around and extended his arms as if he was going to catch her. "Can you hop onto my back?"

Peyton wanted to say no. But she couldn't. After another moment of hesitation, she finally obliged and climbed on his back. She tried not to relish the scent of his leathery aftershave as he carried her through the reeds.

One day, she was going to have quite the story to tell.

If she lived long enough to do so.

"AXEL IS PULLING THE CAR UP," Rocco explained as he carried Peyton through the bristly reeds. Insects revealed their presence by rising around them. Sticks and fallen trees hid beneath muck. Crabs scattered into hiding.

At least Peyton felt as light as a feather on his back. That and her scent brought a strange measure of comfort.

"You guys got here just in time." Peyton sounded breathless. From relief or fear? Or maybe both?

"I went to look for you and couldn't find you. Thankfully, Elise said that she saw you heading downstairs." Rocco tried to keep the edge out of his voice.

It wasn't that he was annoyed. Yet it wasn't that he *wasn't* annoyed either.

The way he was feeling right now was hard to

explain. Slightly perturbed might be the best description. But another part of him was impressed that Peyton had taken the initiative to do what she thought was best.

The woman was clearly spooked. No one could blame her for that. She'd been through an ordeal, and she was here by herself.

Rocco tried to keep those facts at the forefront of his mind as he examined why she was making the decisions she did.

Finally, he reached the gravel lane and lowered Peyton into the backseat of his SUV.

Peyton pressed her eyelids together again. Her ankle clearly hurt.

When he was sure she was secure on the edge of the passenger seat, he knelt in front of her. "I'm going to take your shoe off."

"It's muddy, and it may not smell good." She frowned.

What an odd thing to mention at a time like this. But Rocco ignored it. Perhaps she was a nervous talker.

Carefully, he slid her flat off and ran his fingers across her ankle. "Nothing feels broken."

"That's good." But Peyton still looked tightly

wound, like she might cry out in pain at any moment.

"I'm going to rotate your foot. I need you to tell me if it hurts."

"Oh, I will."

Carefully, Rocco turned her ankle.

Peyton sucked in a quick breath but said nothing.

"I think you're right," Rocco told her. "I don't feel any broken bones. It's probably sprained."

Axel handed him a first aid kit, and Rocco found an ACE bandage inside. Slowly, he began binding Peyton's ankle. He pinned the wrap and straightened.

"That should give it some support and make you feel a little better. Once we get back to Blackout, I'll find you some pain reliever."

Peyton nodded, but her eyes were wide and uncertain. No doubt she hadn't counted on this complication.

Rocco quickly slid her shoe back on, then tucked her inside the SUV and closed the door.

It was time to go talk to Cassidy. She was the police chief here in town. Cassidy's husband, Ty, had already been updated on everything that had happened since he was connected to Blackout.

Colton had asked their friend to give Cassidy a rundown.

Rocco hoped talking to Cassidy would help Peyton feel more at ease.

Then Rocco had some serious questions for her about everything that had happened.

CHAPTER SEVENTEEN

PEYTON COULDN'T STOP THINKING about the feel of Rocco's hand on her leg.

It was stupid. She knew it was.

But she kept thinking about it anyway.

His touch had been so warm, so firm . . . yet tender. The combination disoriented her.

There had been nothing romantic about the way he took care of her. There was nothing romantic about *any* of this.

Just because the man kept stepping in like a knight in shining armor did *not* mean Peyton should fall in love with the guy.

Fall in love?

She still didn't even know if she should completely trust him.

She definitely shouldn't fall in love with him. She shouldn't fall in *like* with him either. She shouldn't even fall in infatuation with him.

There would be no falling here—other than that which occurred when she ran for her life. Peyton would prefer that falling didn't happen either.

It was just one more reason why Peyton needed to stop thinking about how tender the man was, how his accent made her want to melt, and how his smile disarmed her.

What she needed to concentrate on right now was surviving.

They pulled to a stop in front of a police station. They'd done very little talking on the way there, but Rocco had played some classic rock songs on the radio and had sung along with them. As he did, Axel had rolled his eyes in the seat beside him.

The two were quite the pair. Opposites in every way. Rocco was cultured and refined. Axel was rough around the edges and charismatic. Two very different men who were both capable and who could hold their own in a fight.

After Rocco climbed out, he opened the door for Peyton and helped her inside the police station.

As soon as they stepped through the door, a woman wearing a police uniform met them. She appeared to be close to thirty, with blonde hair pulled back into a bun. A warm smile stretched across her face.

"You must be Peyton. I'm Police Chief Cassidy Chambers. Why don't you come and sit in my office?"

Sitting seemed like a good idea.

Rocco released Peyton's arm before nodding at Axel and murmuring, "We'll wait out here for you."

Peyton almost wished Rocco had offered to come with her. But what sense would that make? She needed to ask questions about the man. Doing so in his presence might be uncomfortable, to say the least.

"Why don't you tell me what happened?" Chief Chambers said after they were settled in the office. "I heard a brief rundown. I already have my guys out there looking for the car that chased you."

Peyton launched into today's incident. As she did, the police chief took notes and nodded.

When Peyton finished, Chief Chambers looked up at Peyton and frowned. "You have no idea who might be behind what happened?"

Peyton shook her head. "I have no idea. I'm just as perplexed as everyone else. None of this makes any sense to me."

The chief offered another compassionate smile before leaning with her elbows on her desk toward Peyton. "The good news is, you're in the best place for your protection. You've got some of the top-of-the-line special force officers at your disposal."

Peyton shifted at that statement, wondering exactly how to word her questions so she didn't sound totally ungrateful. "Are you sure I can trust these guys? I mean, one minute I'm delivering cupcakes. The next, I'm being shot at, whisked into a van, and brought to this strange place with people I don't even know. It's all been a bit overwhelming."

The police chief nodded, an empathetic glow in her gaze. "I can imagine. It's a lot for anyone to take in. But I can personally vouch for these guys. They're great, and they're going to take care of you."

"So I can trust them?" Her voice wavered slightly as she asked the question.

"You can definitely trust them. I must say—in full disclosure—that my husband helped to start the organization, so I'm a little biased. But they've helped us out on this island on more than one occasion."

"That's good to know."

The chief pulled something from her drawer. "Here's my card. If there's anything you need—even if it's just another reassurance at some point—feel free to call me. That's my personal line, so it will go right to me."

Peyton looked at the card a moment before sticking it into her pocket. "Thank you. I really appreciate it."

"Like I said earlier, my guys are out there looking for the person who chased you." Chief Chambers offered a confident nod. "In the meantime, just hunker down. Let us do the hard work for you."

Peyton nodded. She already liked the police chief. The woman seemed so down-to-earth and approachable.

Maybe being here under Blackout's protection wasn't as bad as Peyton thought it might be after all.

She stood again and put some weight on her ankle. This time it didn't hurt as bad.

Peyton didn't think she needed crutches. She'd just need to take things slower for a while.

As she left the office, she couldn't help but wonder what else these people targeting her might have in store for her.

ROCCO ROSE to his feet when he saw Peyton emerge from Cassidy's office.

Based on the more relaxed look on her face, the conversation must have gone well.

This could be an act, he reminded himself. Peyton could be in on this. She could be a great actress.

But, somehow, the facts of the case didn't mesh in his mind.

If she was involved, why had she been shot at? Why would she want to talk to the police? Was she trying to earn their trust somehow?

He shook the questions off. He'd have to think on them later.

Cassidy smiled behind Peyton, the action seeming to indicate that his assumption was correct.

"Listen, do you mind if I have a minute with the chief?" Rocco asked. "You can sit on this bench, and I'll be right back."

"Of course."

Rocco nodded and walked with Cassidy toward her office. They didn't bother to step inside. This shouldn't take long.

He lowered his voice. "You heard about that article?"

A frown flickered across her face. "The one about the four gunmen in Norfolk? I did."

"Has anyone come here looking for us?"

"Not yet. The images were blurry."

"There were no cameras in that area, Cassidy."

She squinted. "So where did the footage come from?"

"I have no idea. But it's just a matter of time before authorities track us down."

"I'll keep watch. But if they come . . ." She shrugged.

"I know. You have a duty to report us. Let's hope it doesn't come down to that. Not until we have more answers, at least."

With another nod, Rocco strode back across the room toward Peyton. As she rose, he poised himself to help her if necessary. "Are you walking okay?"

Peyton nodded and slowly moved forward. "I just can't believe I tripped when I was trying to escape. How clichéd."

"When adrenaline kicks in, sometimes we don't think so clearly."

She stole a glance at him. "That obviously wasn't true for you. You were a SEAL."

"Adrenaline makes me sharper. It has to. Otherwise, I would have never gotten through SEAL training. But that's the beautiful part about life. We're all different."

He offered his arm, and Peyton slipped her hand into the crook. Holding on would help give her more balance as she walked toward the door.

"Where's Axel?" She glanced around the station.

"Beckett picked him up. They have some other things they need to do."

"I see."

They continued toward the door then stepped outside.

"Look, I know this restaurant I think you'll really like. Would you like to try it? You're probably hungry."

He wasn't sure where the offer had come from. It just hit him and seemed like a good idea. The plan was for Rocco to get closer to Peyton, and having dinner with her seemed like a good place to start.

Rocco fully expected Peyton to reject the invitation though.

She nodded down at herself. "I'm a little muddy."

"Once you head to the restroom and wash off, you'll be as good as new. Even if you're not, I'm fine with however you look."

Peyton let out a skeptical laugh. To his surprise,

she finally nodded. "Okay. Going to the restaurant seems normal. But are you sure it's safe?"

"Don't worry, I've got your back."

As she looked up at him, her eyes widened. Rocco saw something down deep in the depths of them.

What about his words had caused that reaction? The surprise mixed with a touch of awe and wonder?

He wasn't sure.

But he wanted to know.

And that fact surprised him more than anything.

But the last time he'd allowed himself to get close, the woman he'd loved had just pushed him away at a time when she'd needed him the most.

Would Peyton push him away now also?

And, if she did, wouldn't that simply be for the best?

CHAPTER EIGHTEEN

AS SOON AS Peyton stepped into The Crazy Chefette, she closed her eyes and took a deep breath. The scents of garlic, onions, and Cajun seasoning hit her.

The aromas enticed her, mingling and mixing with memories of times around the table. Graduations. Celebrations. Even times of mourning.

She came out of her trance as Rocco placed his hand on her back. "We can sit over here."

He led her to a table away from the window and then he sat facing the door.

"Looks like a fun place." She glanced around at the quirky decorations. The place had almost been set up like a science lab with beakers and microscopes decorating various surfaces, and it had an overall industrial vibe.

"This is a favorite among locals and foodies. A woman named Lisa Dillinger runs it. She was a chemist until she decided to start experimenting in the kitchen instead of in a laboratory. It seemed like a place that you might like."

"Experimenting in the kitchen, huh?" Peyton had done that a time or two herself.

"She has all kinds of unique food combinations, including a grilled cheese and peach sandwich that people go crazy for."

"That does sound interesting."

He handed her a menu. "You pick whatever you want. It's on me."

"You don't have to do that."

"I don't mind. You've been through a lot, and it's obvious that food is important to you. So treat yourself."

"It's obvious that food is important to me?" She glanced down at her stomach wondering if Rocco had just implied she was overweight.

He grinned. "I know how much *cupcakes* mean to you."

"It's that obvious?"

"It is."

"Cupcakes do make the world a better place."

Rocco chuckled, the sound deep and rumbling. If Peyton had her way, she would listen to it as often as possible. There was something about the sound that filled her soul and warmed her chest.

But she wasn't going to think about that now. Instead, Peyton stared at the menu. The grilled cheese with peaches *did* sound good, but she was in the mood for something else.

After ordering a sandwich with white-pepper-crusted bacon, orange marmalade toast, and baby greens, Peyton glanced at Rocco. Something seemed different about him than before. He almost seemed more guarded. But why?

She'd already wasted too much time in her life questioning people and wondering if she'd done something to offend them.

She'd vowed never to do that again. For that reason, she brushed the feeling off and took a sip of lemonade.

Moving on...

But she knew it was never really that easy.

ROCCO STARED at Peyton across the table.

He just couldn't picture this woman being guilty. It made no sense.

But that video footage didn't lie.

It was clear she had thrown that brick through the glass.

But why? What kind of game was she playing? And how was she so good at making people think she was an innocent victim in all this?

"Do you miss home?" Peyton asked.

He snapped back to the present as the waitress slid a plate across the table. "Home?"

"England? Or wherever you consider home."

"England, usually. And I do sometimes."

She leaned closer. "Have you found any fish and chips here that do the dish justice?"

He fought a smile at her animated, conspiracy-like tone. "Nowhere. It seems a crime, doesn't it?"

"It does." She picked up a fry and took a bite.

"How about you? Are you from Norfolk?"

Her smile dimmed. "A little town called Franklin, Virginia, originally. But I went to college in Norfolk, so I moved in with my brother. It worked out well, especially since my parents left as soon as I graduated."

"What do you mean by left?"

"I'm pretty sure they were counting down the

days until my brother and I were gone." She shrugged. "I don't think parenting was everything they thought it would be."

"Let me guess. You and your brother were little tyrants?"

She shrugged. "Guilty as charged. Not really. I mean, I think I was a pretty easy kid. All the other girls were sneaking off with boys, and I was baking."

He tried to hide his grin but couldn't.

Was this woman simply a fantastic actress? Because she seemed so sincere.

He cleared his throat. He couldn't get lost in this conversation or in Peyton's story. Being guarded was the wisest thing he could do.

"Tell me, have you ever heard of Tartus Enterprises?"

She wiped her mouth and shook her head. "I can't say I have. That's the company that was somehow involved with things last night?"

He nodded. "They were."

"You still don't know what's going on, I guess." She frowned as if she'd been hoping for more.

"We're still looking into things." He didn't tell her that Gabe was going there undercover. He couldn't do that—especially not if Peyton was in on this somehow.

What if that was the case? What if the person selling this tech wanted it to go to the highest bidder? What if someone else had sent Peyton there to prevent the transaction from occurring?

He bit the inside of his lip.

It could have happened. That made the most sense.

But he just didn't want to believe it.

CHAPTER NINETEEN

"THIS WAS DELICIOUS." Peyton pushed her plate away. The food had really been good. She wasn't lying about that.

"I'm glad you enjoyed it." Rocco reached into his pocket and pulled out some bills before tossing them on the table.

"Thank you. I'll pay you back."

"It's no problem."

She thought they would get up to leave, but Rocco remained in his seat, still studying her.

"What happened before I found you today?" he finally asked.

She frowned. She knew this conversation was coming. She just didn't want to talk about it. "I guess

I just freaked out. I realized that I was here on this island with people I didn't know. I don't know who I can trust right now. Everything has been so crazy. I started overthinking it, and I thought what if you guys were actually the bad guys?"

"Then why would we have rescued you?"

"To earn my trust . . . ?" Her voice trailed off in a question. "I mean, there were machine-gun bullets flying, and nobody was hurt. What are the odds?"

"Ever in our favor." The halfway humored expression quickly left his face. "I can see why you might be concerned. But the reason we weren't hit is because we're skilled at what we're doing. We've been in war zones before."

She tugged on the collar of her shirt, suddenly feeling hot. "I know. And I don't mean to sound ungrateful. I really don't. But I know I can be too trusting, and sometimes that makes me swing in the total opposite direction. I question myself and then I stop trusting anyone at all."

She clamped her mouth shut. She shouldn't have said that. If by chance Rocco was the bad guy, then she'd just exposed her weakness. These guys would know exactly where to hit her and what kind of approach would work the easiest.

That all went back to that whole trust issue.

He leaned closer. "Anybody in your shoes would feel uncertain right now. But I'm asking that you trust us. Not forever. Not even for a semi-long time. But just for a few days until we get this sorted out."

She stared at him a moment. At his big brown eyes that held so much sincerity. At his unwavering gaze.

Finally, she nodded. "Okay. For a few days."

ROCCO KEPT TURNING the conversation over in his mind as they drove back to Blackout.

As a trained operative, he knew he needed to dig deeper than what he saw on the surface. But Peyton was very convincing. Almost too convincing.

And that made her dangerous.

He tried to keep his shoulders loose as he headed down the road. He didn't want to raise her suspicions. Yet there was another part of him that wanted to confront her about that video.

Every time he replayed it in his mind, he couldn't forget the look on her face as she'd tossed that brick into her own business. She'd actually smiled.

It was unsettling really.

Peyton let out a long breath, as if trying to focus her thoughts. "So what's up for the rest of the day? Are you going to head back and take a nap?"

"I'm not really a nap taker." Rocco shrugged.

"But you were up all night."

"I've gone six days straight without sleeping."

Her eyes widened. "How is that possible?"

"I remember a time that we were in an undisclosed location. We had insurgents surrounding us the whole time, and it was a battle for our lives. Going to sleep would mean certain death."

She stared at him, something close to awe in her eyes. "How did you even manage to do that? Doesn't your body just break down after a while?"

"We popped caffeine pills. I don't recommend them. But when your life is on the line, sometimes you don't have much choice. After a while you start seeing hallucinations. I've got to say, those aren't good memories. But they make not sleeping right now look like a piece of cake."

He glanced at the streets around them as they traveled, looking for that person who'd followed Peyton in the marsh. Had Axel been able to find him? The man's car had told him nothing. They'd noted the license plate, and, apparently, the vehicle had been stolen from Greensboro yesterday.

But he wasn't ready to give up.

He wasn't sure what was going on.

Was the person chasing Peyton also someone who'd been staged to make Peyton gain Blackout's sympathies? Was she really not in danger at all? Had she been planted inside Blackout as a mole for some reason?

Or, somehow, was there a misunderstanding here? He had trouble seeing how that would be possible. But maybe—just maybe—someone really did want her dead. Maybe, just maybe, someone realized that she had come here to Lantern Beach, and they had followed her.

All those unknown questions made him uncomfortable. Very uncomfortable.

"There's actually a birthday party tonight." Rocco remembered her original question and his order to make friends with her.

"A birthday party? That sounds like fun."

"One of the agents here, Griff, his daughter is turning five. So we're going to have a little party for her in the lobby."

"Do you need cupcakes?" Hopefulness entered her voice.

Rocco glanced at her, trying to gauge whether or not she was sincere. "Really?"

She nodded, her eyes still hopeful and wide. "Really. I would love to make cupcakes. In fact, it would help me keep my mind occupied, which is really what I need right now. Because when I'm alone with nothing to do, all I start doing is thinking."

"I'm sure they would love it if you made cupcakes." He wasn't sure if they had already arranged for some other kind of catering. But according to some people who really love sweets, you could never have too many. And she was right. Making cupcakes would give her something to do and would keep her occupied.

"I'll make sure we have everything that you need, and I'll give you free rein of the kitchen."

She smiled. "That sounds fantastic."

Just as she said the words, Rocco heard something above them.

A *whop whop*.

He glanced up and saw a helicopter coming near them.

His back muscles tightened.

The copter was black, without any logo on the side of it.

The aircraft flew over them. But instead of continuing along, it seemed to swoop lower.

The next moment, Rocco heard gunfire, and his windshield shattered.

CHAPTER TWENTY

"GET DOWN!" Rocco said.

Peyton didn't have to be told twice. She slipped her seatbelt off and crouched on the floor.

Rocco went on full operative mode. His hands gripped the wheel, and his shoulders tightened as he glanced ahead.

Was someone in that helicopter shooting at them? The idea seemed absurd. That seemed like something that might happen in another country. But not here in Lantern Beach.

Wind swept in through the open windshield. Little pieces of glass rained all over her hair and clothing.

But at least she and Rocco hadn't been hit. She could be thankful for that.

As more gunfire rang out, Rocco swerved on the road.

Peyton heard a pop.

Had they shot out one of their tires?

Her heart pounded harder. This was getting worse by the moment.

How were they going to get out of this?

She glanced at Rocco. Even though he was on the defensive, he still acted calm and in control.

Her heart slowed just a little. At least there was that.

He stayed on the road—but just barely.

Another line of gunfire exploded, and the car swerved again.

"We're going to have to get off this road," Rocco said.

"Are you sure that's a good idea?" She lifted her head again.

"We're too wide open out here. We need cover. We need trees."

The next instant, Rocco jerked the wheel. Peyton felt her body shift into the dashboard. She gripped the seat, trying to maintain some type of balance.

But before she could establish that, they were going straight again.

Some type of canopy covered the SUV.

Trees.

Rocco was driving through the woods.

Hopefully, this would protect them from those people in the helicopter.

But if her sense of direction was correct, they were headed for the water. There would be nowhere else they could go down this road.

They could hang out here until the helicopter passed.

And what if the helicopter didn't pass?

The question echoed in her head until her temples began to pound.

AS ROCCO CHARGED down the road, his mind raced.

Whoever was behind these crimes . . . they had money.

And if Peyton really was on their side and not Rocco's, then why have they been shooting at a vehicle while she was inside?

Unless they didn't know she was inside.

But Rocco didn't think that was the case.

He'd have to ponder that later. Right now, he needed to concentrate on surviving.

He still heard the helicopter overhead. He saw its shadow filtering from the trees down onto the road ahead of him.

But the thick branches overhead would allow him a little cover.

Still, a bullet could easily travel through the branches and leaves and into his car.

He gripped the steering wheel tighter.

This was a dead end. He could go only so far. But he also knew that he needed to keep moving.

Movement meant staying alive. Stopping would make them too easy of a target.

But he needed to call for backup. Maybe he could find deeper cover and pull over a moment.

Just up ahead, Rocco saw a small pull-off area in the woods. If he had to guess, a fisherman or hunter had pulled there to park their car at some point while they went on their excursion.

He slipped into the spot, shifted the SUV into Park, and looked at his passenger.

"Are you okay?" Peyton had gone quiet on the floor beside him.

"I think so," she muttered. Terror stained her voice. There was no mistaking that.

The cover over this area was dark. With his SUV being black, they'd blend in a little bit better for a moment. Hopefully long enough to make this call.

Colton answered the phone, and Rocco explained the situation to him.

"I'm on it," Colton said. "Stay safe."

Rocco ended the call and then listened.

The helicopter seemed to be getting quieter.

Could it be?

He glanced out the window and saw the helicopter was moving away.

What was that about?

Except maybe whoever was piloting that helicopter knew they couldn't stay in the air very long. They had to know that authorities were going to question who was in their air space and would send somebody to check it out.

Maybe they were retreating before that happened.

But he felt certain the copter hadn't come from this island. There were only a few places that it could land here.

As the sound of the copter faded, he looked down at Peyton again. "You can get up now."

She glanced at him with her eyes wide. But after a moment, she emerged from the cocoon she had put herself in on the floor. Shards of glass continued to rain down around her, but she brushed them onto the floor.

Against his better instincts, Rocco reached for her and squeezed her arm. The next instant, she leaned into his shoulder as trembles overtook her.

CHAPTER TWENTY-ONE

BACK AT THE BLACKOUT HEADQUARTERS, Rocco checked Peyton for any injuries. But Peyton knew she was fine.

On the outside at least.

On the inside, she felt like a hot mess. But she couldn't let herself fall apart.

Her life had flashed before her eyes back there.

Again.

How many times could that happen within two days?

At least three, she realized.

Rocco and Colton murmured to themselves for a few minutes before Rocco turned back to her. "Listen, I have some things I need to do. How about if I set you up in the kitchen so you can bake? Or would you rather lie down?"

She didn't even have to think about her answer. "Bake. Definitely."

He nodded as if he'd expected that answer. "Let me show you where to go then."

He placed a hand on the small of her back and gently led her down the hallway to the kitchen.

Her eyes lit up when she saw the commercial-sized area.

She could really have a lot of fun in here. This might be just what she needed to get rid of some of her stress.

After Rocco showed her around and made sure she had all the cupcake ingredients she needed, he turned to her again. His eyes examined her as if trying to ascertain her state of mind.

"You're sure you're okay?" His gaze narrowed as he studied her without apology.

She really wasn't sure about anything, but she nodded anyway. "I'll be okay. Thanks for not getting us killed back there."

A smile curled only part of his lips, but then it quickly disappeared. "I'll be back and check on you in a little while."

She nodded. "I'll look forward to it."

I'll look forward to it?

Horror washed over her.

Had she just flirted?

This whole situation was definitely messing with her psyche.

She only hoped her cupcakes would fix that as well.

ROCCO SPENT the next hour on the phone with air traffic control. They were trying to track down the operator of that helicopter. So far, they'd had no luck. The helicopter was now nowhere to be seen.

Beckett was looking into anyone who owned a helicopter in the area. Unfortunately, Rocco hadn't seen any type of numbers on the aircraft that would help identify it. If he had to guess, the chopper was probably parked somewhere over on the mainland.

The one thing that didn't make sense to him was why someone would shoot at them while Peyton was in the car.

If she was involved with this, then it made no sense to try to kill her.

It was another piece of the puzzle that didn't fit.

Rocco lowered his head as he felt the pounding begin there again.

He reached into his desk and pulled out his migraine medicine. He'd only started suffering from migraines after his last mission. Some type of gas had been sprayed on them, and now each team member had lasting effects from whatever it had been.

The military had yet to identify exactly what was in that chemical spray. Maybe they never would.

Rocco had to get control of his migraine before it overtook him. If he wasn't careful, it could debilitate him until he could do nothing but lie in bed in a dark room.

For a former SEAL, that was hard for him to stomach. He liked to be out in the field. Liked to be the one hunting down bad guys. Liked stopping people before they did things that could hurt others.

He drank the rest of his water and sat there for a moment, trying to even his breathing.

But this had been a long day. A very long day, and there were no signs it was going to get shorter anytime soon.

Beckett popped his head into Rocco's office. "Rocco, could you join us for a minute?"

"Of course."

He followed his colleague down the hallway and into a conference room. The rest of his team was already there. A bad feeling gripped Rocco's stomach when he saw them.

"What's going on?" He pulled out a seat and waited to hear what everybody else already appeared to know.

Colton frowned before saying, "We just received word that John Belching is dead."

Rocco blanched at the stark words. Certainly, he hadn't heard his friend correctly. "What?"

Colton nodded, not bothering to hide the somberness on his face. "I just heard. He died a week ago."

John had been a member of another SEAL team, but they'd all worked with the man on multiple occasions.

"What happened?" Rocco held his breath as he waited to hear the details.

Colton drew in another deep breath before explaining. "He was in a car accident."

"What?" Rocco shook his head, still reeling at the announcement.

"I'm sorry. I know this is a lot to process."

Rocco ran a hand over his face, still unable to comprehend the death of another SEAL. "That's terrible. He hasn't even been out of the military that long, and he was trying so hard to rebuild his life."

"I know." Colton rubbed his jaw, a storm of grief brewing in his gaze. "We can't believe it either." He shifted. "I figured we should let you know. Just in case..."

Rocco's spine stiffened. "Just in case what?"

"Just in case this turns out to be anything more than a car accident." Colton frowned.

"Is that what you think it was?" Axel leaned forward, lines forming across his forehead. "Or should I ask: is that *really* what you think it was?"

"I don't know." Colton's gaze traveled from Axel to Beckett, then finally Rocco. "We know as Navy SEALs we have a lot of enemies. Every time a SEAL dies, it's worth pausing, not only to grieve but to wonder if it's the work of one of our enemies."

"Is someone planning a funeral?" Rocco hated to ask the question, but he had to. Someone needed to honor the man's life, and, as far as he knew, John didn't have any living relatives.

"As soon as we hear something, I'll let you know."

"Please, do that." Rocco didn't want to bury another one of his friends. He knew it was the nature of the work they did. The situations they faced were dangerous.

But death never got easier. Rocco never wanted it to. He never wanted his heart to harden to tragedy.

Colton leaned forward and sighed. "I'd love to keep talking about John. But right now, we have other pressing matters at hand. We need to talk about everything that happened last night and see if we can figure out a plan. I was hoping more evidence and answers would have turned up by now, but they haven't. That means we need to buckle down even more."

CHAPTER TWENTY-TWO

PEYTON NEEDED to do something to relieve her stress. She could feel it building inside her, and the last thing she needed was to have a breakdown.

Baking was a great start. She could lose herself in the process. It almost seemed disrespectful to try to enjoy herself after what just happened. But she had to unwind.

She pulled out all the ingredients and pans she needed to bake. Then she found an old radio in the corner and turned it on.

This would be perfect.

As she started mixing her batter, her mind continually went back to the sound of that helicopter overhead. Then she remembered the sound of the bullets. The glass breaking. How she could feel the danger in the air.

She shivered.

If anybody other than Rocco had been driving, she might not be alive right now. Certainly, if Peyton had been the one driving, she wouldn't be alive right now.

She shivered again.

Just as she iced her last cupcake, someone else stepped into the kitchen.

She glanced up and saw ... Rocco.

Her heart quickened at the sight of him.

Because he was a friendly face, of course.

Baking three dozen cupcakes had also helped.

He paused near her and crossed his arms, leaning with his hip against the counter as he watched her. "You look like you're having fun."

"Baking is just what the doctor ordered."

"I'm glad to hear that."

She picked up a platter she'd put together. "Would you like to try one? Maybe this is just what the doctor ordered for you."

"I probably shouldn't." He patted his flat stomach.

"Just one won't hurt. What kind do you like? Chocolate on chocolate? Vanilla with chocolate icing? Or maybe chocolate with vanilla icing? I was going to make strawberry, but I didn't have the ingredients for that one."

"Chocolate on chocolate. For sure."

Peyton found one on the tray and handed it to him and then watched as he took a bite.

Rocco's eyes widened as he chewed and swallowed. "These *are* good."

She shrugged, trying not to show how satisfied she felt at his words. "Thank you. That's exactly what I like to hear."

"I'm sure Ada will be thrilled."

"I hope so."

Peyton knew she should ask him for an update on everything that had happened. Yet, for just a little longer, she wanted to escape all of that. Maybe even pretend it hadn't happened.

As a new song began playing on the radio, her heart lifted.

"'Sweet Caroline!' I *love* this song." She twirled in a circle before swaying back and forth with the chorus.

As she sang along, she glanced at Rocco and saw his eyes glinted with amusement.

"What? You don't like to dance when you listen to your favorite songs?"

"I'll never tell." Dry humor laced his voice.

Peyton paused in front of him and sang another line, embracing the brief moment of normalcy.

"You know you just want to burst out into a dance," she goaded him.

"Is that right?" He continued to stare.

The next instant, he began belting along with the song and imitating her dance moves.

The sight of it made her double over with laughter.

Rocco *did* have a sense of humor. She laughed so hard that Rocco stepped toward her and gripped the side of her arms as if checking to see if she was okay.

Peyton drew in a deep breath, trying to pull herself together. But when she looked up at Rocco, her heart seemed to stop.

Okay. She could stop denying it.

She was *definitely* attracted to this man. Even if this was the absolute worst time to be attracted to anybody.

Still, it was the truth. The man was handsome and kind, *and* he had a killer accent.

Their gazes caught a moment, and she sucked in a breath.

Did Rocco feel the same way? Or was Peyton just a job to him?

Based on the emotions she saw swirling in his gaze, he felt something also.

Her relationship with Rodger slammed into her mind. All the mistakes she'd made. The way she'd nearly given up on her dreams because of the way he'd mocked her and made her doubt herself.

She'd vowed never to put herself in a situation like that again.

Was Rocco one of those guys who needed to make others feel small so he could feel more powerful?

She didn't think so.

But she had to be sure.

Peyton quickly looked away before Rocco noticed any attraction in her gaze. She cleared her throat as she turned around and saw the mess she'd made.

"I guess I should get cleaned up here," she murmured.

Rocco stepped back also, seeming to snap out of his daze. "Let me help."

Peyton's cheeks heated at the thought of being around him more. Yet another part of her craved it. "Are you sure?"

"I'm sure. But we better get busy."

"CAN I HAVE A WORD WITH YOU?"

Rocco looked up as someone new stepped into the kitchen.

Colton.

Working with Peyton in the kitchen had been a nice distraction.

As had staring into her eyes. Watching her smile as she sang along to "Sweet Caroline." Feeling her hands against his arms.

He hadn't felt a rush of attraction like that in such a long time.

Since Natalie . . .

He dried his hands, still wet from washing dishes, and glanced at Peyton. He needed to get his thoughts under control. This was no time to think about anything other than finding answers. He chided himself for enjoying himself at a time like this.

He should be in mourning over his friends. Be cautious over everything that had transpired. Be fired up and ready to fight at a moment's notice.

"Excuse me a minute." His voice sounded raspier than he'd expected as he turned to Peyton.

She nodded and continued drying a bowl, humming as she did.

Rocco strode across the room and followed Colton into the lobby. No one else was around.

"You two look like you're having fun." Colton's voice was a mix of curiosity and caution.

"You mean fun washing dishes?"

Colton shrugged. "I peeked in on you two a little bit earlier. It looked like more than dishwashing that was taking place."

Rocco chuckled and shook his head a little too quickly. "I think you're reading too much into things."

Sure, Rocco had felt a spark. But that didn't mean he planned on acting on it.

"If I didn't know better, I'd think she seemed like a nice girl." Colton frowned, no doubt remembering that video of her throwing the brick.

Rocco felt the same way. What he'd experienced face-to-face with Peyton and what he'd seen on that video were two vastly different things. He had trouble reconciling them.

Rocco glanced back at the kitchen door, hoping to catch another glimpse of her. "Peyton is definitely different."

"Different good or different bad?"

He remembered hearing Peyton sing in the kitchen as she made her cupcakes. "Different good. She's a breath of fresh air, I suppose. Then again, I'm used to being around all you stuffy guys."

Colton chuckled before shaking his head and turning back to the conversation.

Rocco hadn't been able to distract him.

"I'm not judging either way," Colton said. "I'm just saying it's nice to see you smile again. I haven't seen you look that comfortable with somebody since Natalie."

At the mention of Natalie's name, Rocco's heart stilled.

Colton didn't know what he was talking about. Natalie had been one of a kind. There'd never been anyone else like her.

Yet she'd broken his heart. When Natalie had needed him the most, she'd pushed Rocco away.

And now there was no going back to make things right.

That fact would always haunt him.

"Peyton and I were just trying to unwind after a horrendous day," Rocco said. "Besides, it's not like I can hit on someone when I'm working on a case."

"Yet Peyton hasn't officially hired us . . . food for thought." Colton raised his eyebrows. "I might even encourage it—if it wasn't for the fact she's also a suspect."

"Good to know. For a minute, I thought you were encouraging me to date a woman with unknown intentions and involvement in our case."

"No, but it is good to see you relaxing a little. Gives me hope that one day you'll be as happy as I am."

"Yeah, well, you and Elise are pretty much perfect together. We can't all be that lucky." Rocco didn't want to talk about this any longer. There were more important matters at hand, and they both knew it. "Is this why you stopped by?"

The smile disappeared from Colton's face as he turned dead serious. "I wish it was. But, no, it's not. I wanted to let you know that Branson is coming in later tonight. He wants to talk face to face about what happened."

"A phone call wouldn't do, huh?"

"He's very concerned. And, honestly, I'm anxious to talk to him also. I want to look him in the eye and find out what's really going on here. He didn't give us much information about this proprietary technology at the center of all this. But if someone is this desperate to get their hands on it, then it really does make me wonder."

"Me too," Rocco said. "Do you know when he's arriving?"

"Right after Ada's birthday party."

"Perfect. I'll be ready."

"But whatever you do, we're not going to ruin this little girl's birthday party for work."

"I would never even think about it."

"Good," Colton said. "Because it starts in one hour."

CHAPTER TWENTY-THREE

AS PEYTON STOOD at the edge of the crowd, she watched the princess-themed party coming to life around her.

The "royal ballroom" had been set up outside not too far from the water. Party lights had been strung over a wooden platform, and fun Disney music played on speakers from somewhere.

Little Ada, whom Peyton had just met, was dressed in a teal princess gown and sparkly crown. The girl made her way through the crowd, blessing everyone she came in contact with.

The sight was adorable.

But Peyton had to admit that she felt out of place. These people around her were like family to each other. Peyton was just a temporary addition. At least, that's what she hoped.

She longed to get back to her old life.

But would her old life ever be the same?

She didn't know the answer to that question.

Certainly, the past twenty-four hours had changed her. Opened her eyes to the danger around her. To possible betrayal. To grief.

And then there was Rocco . . . how would she ever be able to forget about him?

The man put guys like Rodger to shame. More than anything Peyton wanted to trust her gut instinct, which told her that Rocco was indeed one of the good guys. She wanted to believe he was nothing like Rodger. That maybe there were guys out there with noble intentions.

Wasn't that what she wanted? Someone who believed in her? Someone who could be her best friend but also sweep her off her feet?

Maybe she still had a little bit of Ada inside her. Maybe dressing like a princess and hoping for all the best things for the future was still alive somewhere deep inside her.

Her gaze wandered across the crowd until she saw Rocco. As she remembered the impromptu dance they'd shared earlier, her cheeks flushed. She really shouldn't be so impulsive. But she would be lying if she said she didn't enjoy it.

She'd even enjoyed cleaning up with Rocco. As they'd worked, he'd told her stories about growing up in England, including tales about his family. They sounded like people Peyton would like to meet. His upbringing was so much different than hers.

She was pretty sure her parents had stumbled into parenthood, discovered they didn't like it, and counted down the days until Peyton and Anderson became adults. Her mother was a photographer, and her father made homemade guitars.

Last time she'd heard from them, they'd been in Costa Rica.

She watched Rocco now. He'd changed into a suit. His hair looked neat and clean. He mixed and mingled with the crowd, smiling at everyone and making them laugh.

She quickly looked away before anybody caught her staring. As she did, her gaze went to the table where the cupcakes had been displayed.

About half of them were already gone, and Peyton had received rave compliments from everyone who'd tried one. The accolades never got old. Using her skills to make other people happy was one of the highlights of her life.

"Attention." Ada tapped her fork against a glass until everyone looked at her.

Peyton smiled at the sight of the girl. She was a go-getter. Peyton already liked her.

"Now, we're going to have the princess dance. Everyone needs to find a partner." She glanced around and her sweet expression turned serious—dramatically so. "I mean it."

Peyton's hand flew over her mouth to hide a smile.

Yes, she *definitely* liked this little five-year-old.

Giggles went through the crowd as couples began to slow dance together.

Peyton stepped farther back into the shadows, really feeling like an intruder now.

As much as she loved watching Ada stand on her father's shoes as they swayed on a makeshift dance floor, another part of her realized that she shouldn't be here.

In fact, maybe she should disappear into her room for a while and get some rest. After all, she had hardly slept today.

Yes, that was what she would do. She would slip away.

Peyton took a step back into the darkness when a

deep voice called out to her. "Would you like to dance?"

She turned and saw Rocco standing there.

Her cheeks flushed at the sight of him. She really wished they'd stop doing that.

She swallowed hard before asking, "Are you just asking because you feel sorry for me because I'm a loner over here?"

"I'm asking because there's a birthday girl who requested we all dance, and I need a partner."

Peyton remained still another moment, trying to read Rocco's expression before she finally nodded. "Okay then."

She tried not to show her nerves as Rocco put one hand on her waist and took her other hand in his. They stood a comfortable distance from each other as they swayed back and forth to the sound of "One Day My Prince Will Come."

Peyton held back a bitter laugh. She used to believe that. She used to believe her Prince Charming was out there. She was the ultimate optimist.

In so many ways, she still was. But not when it came to love. She'd been burned too badly.

"You look lovely tonight," Rocco said.

She glanced down at the black dress that

Bethany had loaned her. It had fit surprisingly well, as had the black heels. "Thank you."

They swayed quietly for a few minutes before Rocco asked, "Have you ever been married, Peyton?"

Her eyes widened in surprise at his question. "No, I haven't."

"Ever been close?"

She felt tension swell inside her. She hardly ever talked about Rodger. But there was no need to hide from the truth. Her past had made her who she was today.

"I was engaged one time. But thankfully I came to my senses and called it off."

"Why was that?" He stared down at her, his eyes looking warm as the party lights reflected in them.

From some people, the questions might sound intrusive. But coming from Rocco, it seemed like a casual conversation. Not only that, but she had the undeniable urge to reach up and run her fingers down his beard. She wondered if it felt as soft as she thought it did.

She cleared her throat, chiding herself for the thought.

"Rodger and I met when I helped cater an event for his startup company," she began. "He was everything I wasn't: confident, strong, charismatic. In fact, and this is going to sound silly, but he insisted that people not call him Rodger. They called him Dger."

"Dger? Like the second syllable of his name?" Rocco's eyebrows shifted together.

She nodded and let out a laugh. "Believe me, I know. It's weird."

"I'd say, *Yton*."

She giggled again. "Anyway, he pursued me hard, and I'm sorry to say I fell for it. But I came to realize over time that I felt myself shrinking around him."

A wrinkle formed between Rocco's brow. "What do you mean?"

"I don't mean I physically shrank. It wasn't that Rodger was physically abusive. But he always talked down to me, especially when referring to 'my little cupcake business.' It was like if he let me shine then he felt like his light would be diminished."

"That's too bad."

"It was hard. But breaking up with him was the best thing. Marrying him would have only brought me misery."

They continued to sway to the music. "That's what it sounds like. My mum used to always say that one of the best gifts you can give somebody is letting them be themselves. That's always stuck with me."

Peyton thought about those words for a minute.

"I like that advice. Too many times people meet somebody, and they want to change all the things they don't like about the person. It's not that we can't become better versions of ourselves. But accepting somebody as they are is a great gift."

Rocco smiled. "I agree."

Peyton let out a breath, relaxing some more. "So you know a little bit about my love life. What about yours?"

Some of the brightness left his eyes. "Never been married. But I wanted to get married."

Peyton had a hard time believing anybody would ever break up with him. But there was obviously a story there. "Did she break your heart?"

He shrugged, somberness surrounding him. "Her name was Natalie. When I met her, I knew she had a heart condition. Doctors weren't sure how long she would live. There was no treatment for it, and she kept trying to push me away. But I wouldn't let her. It didn't matter how much time I had with her, I would take anything I could get."

Peyton's heart pounded in her ears as she listened to his story. "What happened?"

"I eventually convinced her to date me. We were together for a year, and I wanted to marry her, but she wouldn't have anything to do with it. Especially since her heart condition seemed to be getting worse."

Peyton remained quiet, listening to his every word.

"In fact, Natalie broke up with me. The next day, I was sent to the Middle East for a month-long mission. She wouldn't take my calls or respond to my texts. Her mom called me three weeks into my mission to let me know she'd died. The doctor had told her it was coming, and that was why she broke up with me. She didn't want to put me through that."

"I am so sorry." Peyton's voice sounded raspy, and tears glistened in her eyes.

"Me too. I'm grateful for the time I had with her. I wanted to be there for her when she needed me the most, but she wouldn't let me. I should have fought harder. Been more convincing."

"But it was her choice. You can't blame yourself for that."

"Love is supposed to cast out fears." Rocco's jaw hardened.

"It sounds like she was trying to protect you..."

"I wanted to protect her. I know no one can really protect someone from a life-threatening illness. But I wish she'd trusted me. I wish we'd had the chance to talk, to make things right before..."

Peyton stepped closer as her hand trailed to meet his. "I'm sorry."

They continued to dance, not saying anything for another moment. But the conversation lingered in Peyton's mind.

There was much more to Rocco Foster than she thought.

Though she didn't like to hear about his pain, she was fascinated with the person beneath his tough veneer.

Maybe a little too fascinated.

AS THE SONG ended and Rocco stepped away, he immediately missed the closeness he'd shared with Peyton.

The realization surprised him.

He felt a surge of protectiveness as she'd told him about her ex. He'd met that type before and knew exactly the kind of guy Peyton was talking about.

Rocco was so glad that Peyton had come to her senses before marrying that man. Someone like that would have just used Peyton. He would have been supposedly committed to her while having flings on the side.

Rocco had also surprised himself by opening up about Natalie. He hardly ever talked about her. But telling his story had just felt right.

He had vowed to never fall in love again. Not after having something so special with Natalie. But what if there was somebody else out there who could make him just as happy?

He didn't know. And he wasn't expecting to think about that right now.

In fact, he especially didn't need to think about this with Peyton.

All the details of what was going on with her collided in his mind. There was the video he saw of her breaking that window herself. If she was somehow involved, then why were the men in that helicopter trying to shoot her? That question continued to linger in his mind.

It didn't make any sense. He wanted to feel peace about the situation. He wasn't at that point yet.

And if Colton hadn't told Rocco not to ask Peyton about the video, Rocco would do exactly that. He wanted answers. He wanted to know if Peyton could be trusted or not.

"Thank you for the dance." Peyton looked up at him with wide eyes that held so much authenticity.

People couldn't fake that, could they? That salt-of-the-earth goodness?

The woman was undeniably beautiful. She also seemed so innocent, like the type who couldn't lie and get away with it. No, she seemed like the type who would lie and it would be written all over her face because she was so terrible at it. And Rocco was generally a pretty good judge of character.

Rocco cleared his throat, trying to get his thoughts under control. "It was a nice dance. Thank you."

Still standing beside each other, they turned to look back at Ada and to wait for her next instructions.

Before the girl could speak, a sound filled the air.

A *whop-whop-whop*.

Peyton clutched his arm.

Another helicopter?

Rocco prayed this one wasn't coming back armed with guns and flying bullets.

CHAPTER TWENTY-FOUR

FEAR OVERTOOK Peyton when she saw the helicopter. When she remembered their earlier ordeal. When she recalled how her life had flashed before her eyes.

She held her breath, at any minute expecting to hear the bullets flying.

Bullets?

Peyton's gaze shot toward Ada.

The girl stood with her father, staring at the sky.

Someone needed to protect her. To protect the innocent child.

What if—

Rocco squeezed her arm. "It's okay. That's one of our clients coming in for a visit."

"What?" Had Peyton heard him correctly?

"I just got a text from Colton about it." He held up his phone. "This is actually the man who hired us for the assignment last night. He wants to come to discuss things face-to-face. But he ended up getting here a bit earlier than he'd told us."

Peyton's heart rate slowed ever so slightly. "I see. That's good. I'm glad."

"Colton is going to go meet him, but the rest of us are staying here until this party is done. That's what we promised each other we would do."

"That makes a lot of sense to me." She fought a smile. She admired someone who could put a promise to a little girl above a security issue.

In fact, she was starting to like Rocco more and more. Definitely more than she anticipated. When she first met him, she thought he was a handsome Neanderthal type of guy. She'd been so wrong.

Peyton couldn't get over the story about him and the woman he'd loved. But she wasn't surprised. Rocco seemed like just that type who would be faithful and loyal no matter the circumstances.

But all those warm fuzzy feelings only delayed reality.

Somebody was trying to kill her.

Peyton had nowhere to go except this facility in

the middle of nowhere with these strangers who were almost beginning to feel like friends.

But this safety net couldn't last forever.

What would happen when it was jerked out from beneath her?

ROCCO MADE sure that Peyton was safely in her room with a phone charger—as she requested—before heading downstairs to meet with Branson.

He was anxious for answers about what was going on, and he hoped Branson might be able to provide some.

Rocco had met the man once before. Though the guy was immersed in the technology world, Branson looked more like a cowboy with his boots, jeans, and Western shirts. He acted like a cowboy too.

He wasn't exactly the kind of guy that Rocco would want to sit down and have coffee with either. He was a touch arrogant and a touch paranoid. Between those two things, conversations were exhausting.

Rocco joined the rest of the guys in the conference room.

"Just the person we were waiting for." Colton sat up straighter when he walked in.

Rocco nodded a polite hello to Branson. "Glad you made it."

"I wish I could say I was glad to be here," Branson muttered, his eyes narrowed as if he were already annoyed.

Rocco and Colton exchanged a glance. An unhappy client was never good. Rocco knew this ultimately fell on his shoulders. He'd been in charge of that mission that had gone wrong.

Colton straightened some papers in his hands before passing them around to everyone at the table and beginning the meeting. "I want to start with Rocco giving his version of the events that played out last night."

Rocco cleared his throat and launched into what had happened. When he finished, Branson shook his head like a coach whose team had just lost the Super Bowl.

"Who was the woman who walked into the middle of things?" Branson demanded.

"Her name is Peyton Ellison," Rocco said. "Does that name sound familiar to you at all?"

Rocco hadn't wanted to say her name. Didn't want to bring her up. But it was important that they knew if Branson had any connection to her, especially considering that video.

"Never heard of her before," Branson muttered. "Should I have?"

"We can't find any apparent connections between her and you," Rocco said. "Her brother is a guy named Anderson Ellison. Does that name sound familiar?"

A knot formed on Branson's brow as he pressed his lips together. "No. Not at all."

Rocco hadn't found any connection between them, but he'd wanted to ask anyway.

Branson shifted in his seat. "I don't know what's going on here, but I don't like it. I need to find out who the mole is in my company. I need to find out who is trying to take this technology that I've put years and years of my life into and sell it to the highest bidder."

"We're doing our best," Colton reassured him.

"We don't have time for any mistakes. If somebody else releases this tech before I do, then I'm done. I'm bankrupt, broke, and my company is going to shut down. More than a hundred people will lose their jobs. There's more on the line than my ego here."

"We understand that." Colton's voice contained a

professional edge as he addressed Branson's concerns. "We're doing everything that we know to find out what is going on here. Is there anything you're not telling us that we should know about?"

Rocco held his breath as he waited to hear what Branson had to say.

Would the man offer any type of answer?

Or would this whole meeting be for nothing?

CHAPTER TWENTY-FIVE

PEYTON DIDN'T WANT to go to sleep until her phone got enough charge for her to check her messages.

Twenty minutes later, the screen came on. She lay in her bed, holding the plugged-in device in her hands.

After it booted up, she scrolled through her emails. She saw nothing of interest there.

But a moment later, a message popped up telling her she had a new voicemail.

What had she missed? She felt disconnected from her old life, which in some ways might be good. In other ways, she wanted to know what was going on. That wasn't to mention the fact that she had orders to fill.

She needed to get on the phone and start calling some of her customers to let them know that she was going to be tied up for a while. She hated to do that to them. Her business was built on being both creative and responsible.

But Peyton didn't know what else she could do right now. Even if she could make treats in the kitchen here, it wasn't like she could drive them the entire four-hour trip up to Norfolk to deliver them. Thankfully, she knew a couple of other bakers in the area who might be able to help her out.

But a moment later, her brother's voice came over her phone line.

"Peyton, it's Anderson. I hate to tell you this over voicemail, but you're not answering your phone. I'm getting worried. Anyway, I've been trying to get up with Suzy all day so I could figure out why she made that phone call to you. But nobody has seen her. I think . . . I think she's missing. I'm not sure what's going on, but you need to be careful. Very careful."

Peyton played the message again to make sure she'd understood correctly.

Karen was dead and now Suzy was missing? Two people who were directly connected with her had either been killed or were in danger.

She dropped her head back onto her pillow.

None of this made any sense. There was no reason to harm people connected with her. There was no reason to harm Peyton.

So why was all this happening?

Could Rodger be connected with this in some way? He was the only person Peyton could think of who had a reason to hate her. He didn't take their breakup well. But she hadn't heard from the man in at least three or four months. In fact, she'd heard rumors he was already seeing somebody else.

The questions continued to throb in her head.

She rose to her feet. She knew that Rocco was occupied with something, but he'd want to hear this. Suzy's disappearance could be in some way connected with everything that had happened. Peyton didn't want to wait until morning to tell him just in case it was important.

Decision made, Peyton stood.

She'd run downstairs and try to find Rocco, tell him the news, and then she would leave that information in his capable hands.

Plus, the idea of seeing him again made this grim situation seem just a little brighter.

BRANSON LEANED BACK in his seat and announced, "This technology that everyone is anxious to get their hands on? It's a dictation app."

Rocco stared at the man, unsure if he had heard everything correctly. "Why would terrorists or other criminals want to get their hands on something that was simply a dictation app? It just doesn't make any sense."

"It's a really good dictation app," Branson said. "You can train it, and the program will accurately pick up on everything you say. This kind of technology will save people a lot of time and energy. I'm telling you—it's going to be the wave of the future. There are other apps out there, but not like this."

Rocco would have to take his word for it. Even if this app was as good as Branson said, it sounded like something another tech company might want to get their hands on.

Not a terrorist.

Those guys with machine guns definitely didn't seem like techies from Cupertino.

Something just didn't make sense about the whole situation.

"Do you have any idea who might be behind this?" Axel asked, beating Rocco to the question.

"I have it narrowed down to five employees I

think are most likely responsible." Branson paused, his jaw flexing before he spoke again. "The thing is, most of my employees only work on one aspect of this technology. I planned that on purpose so that nobody would have access to the complete design. If one of my employees only knows part of the technology, it would do them no good."

Rocco had to admit that his plan seemed wise. "It makes sense that you've scattered pieces so someone doesn't have all the power. So who are these suspects?"

Branson pushed a paper toward them. "I've written them all out. These are the higher-ups in the company. The ones who might be able to go to the individual employees and try to piece together something. They're smart enough to do that. I don't want to think about any of them betraying me, but it is a possibility."

"We'll look into each of these people," Colton assured him. "In the meantime, as you know, we placed our employee Gabe within your business. He's going to listen to the scuttlebutt and see what he can find out."

"Yes, Gabe. Very bright young man. I showed him around the office today and introduced him to people. I'm hoping he'll find out something."

Colton placed his iPad on the table and leaned back. "That's what we're hoping too. Because once we know who is trying to sell the product, then we can find out who they are trying to sell it to. There's a good chance that they have people competing for this. And in that case, I could see where danger would be stirred up."

"I agree." Branson leaned back as if he had another thought. "This woman, the one who walked onto the scene and ruined your operation? Are you sure she's not connected to this somehow?"

Rocco remembered that video he'd seen of Peyton with a brick.

His gaze met Colton's as he contemplated what to say.

Branson had hired them to do a job. It wouldn't be fair of them to withhold the truth from the man.

Yet Rocco didn't want to say anything.

He had to make a decision, and he needed to make it quickly.

CHAPTER TWENTY-SIX

AS PEYTON PAUSED outside the conference room door, voices floated out.

"Are you sure that she's not connected to this somehow?" an unfamiliar voice asked.

She knew she should push her way inside and announce her presence. But she'd frozen.

Whoever was in that room . . . they were talking about her, weren't they?

Peyton's pulse pounded in her ears as she waited to hear the response. She waited for a denial. The Blackout guys knew the truth. They knew she was innocent in this.

"We are looking into her background to make sure that she's not connected in any way to this."

Rocco's unmistakable British accent floated through the air.

Peyton released her breath, feeling a moment of relief. That was what she'd expected him to say. Of course, they'd looked into her background. It was only responsible.

"As of right now, there's nothing pointing to the fact that she would be involved in this in any way," Rocco continued. "Nothing except..."

Peyton's lungs tightened again. Except? There were exceptions?

"We did find a security video of Peyton breaking the window to her bakery right before she left on the evening of our operation," Rocco said.

Peyton suppressed a gasp. What was he talking about? Was he trying to make himself look better by making her look guilty? To somehow make him seem more competent to the people who'd hired him?

Outrage filled her. How could she have been so foolish? Just an hour earlier, she was marveling that Rocco was one of the good guys.

Peyton had been wrong. So, so wrong.

Again.

When would she ever learn that she couldn't trust her instincts, especially when it came to men?

Maybe she'd *never* learn that lesson.

Which might be why she would simply be better off single.

Sadness pressed into her, deep and heavy, almost as if she'd betrayed herself and now had to face the repercussions. How could she have been so stupid?

Peyton drew in a deep breath and straightened her spine.

She couldn't stay here and pretend like she trusted these guys. What if they were just keeping her on campus to make sure she wasn't guilty?

Or to *set her up* as being guilty?

Peyton didn't know the answers to any of those questions. But they were ones she needed to address.

For now, she fled back to her room.

She couldn't talk to any of these people. Not now.

And if she was smart, she'd never open up or try to trust them again.

Especially Rocco.

ROCCO DROVE Branson to a property outside of Blackout to stay for the evening.

It wasn't their practice to let just anybody stay on

campus. Their grounds were secure, and even letting a client stay here would open them up for more risk. Especially after a security breach they'd had not too long ago when someone had killed a newly hired maintenance worker and come in his place. They had to be extra careful.

Of course, Peyton had been the exception. When they had taken Peyton in, it was because they feared she was in danger.

Now that video had surfaced, which made Rocco question that decision. Despite his doubts, he was at peace knowing that Peyton was safer here than she would be anywhere else.

He hated telling Branson about the video, but he didn't feel right keeping it to himself either. The man deserved to know the truth about the situation.

"So you're going to look into this Peyton woman some more?" Branson asked as they headed down the road.

Rocco hadn't told the man that Peyton was staying on the campus. It was better that way. Besides, there was no reason Branson needed to know that.

"We're going to explore every possible suspect," Rocco said. "Thank you for giving us a list of possible moles within your company. As soon as we can single out the person trying to sell your technology, we'll be able to question them and figure out who they're trying to sell it to. Your product should be safe."

Branson nodded. "Good. That's what I like to hear. You probably think I'm just a greedy entrepreneur. But I'm not. I worked hard to get to where I am. It's not fair for somebody else to take credit for what I developed."

"That's understandable." Rocco meant the words.

"You guys came highly recommended to me." Branson shifted, resting one cowboy boot over his leg. "I hope you don't let me down. I'm counting on all of you."

"We're doing everything within our power to figure this out. We'll keep you in the loop." Rocco stopped in front of the man's rental house.

Branson lowered his head, peering at Rocco through narrow eyes. "You better."

The man climbed out and grabbed his bag from the back. "I've got this. You just get back to your headquarters and figure out who's behind this."

Rocco wished it was that easy. He wished he

could just plug in a formula or do a quick internet search that would turn up all the answers.

But it wasn't that easy.

It never was.

CHAPTER TWENTY-SEVEN

EVEN THOUGH PEYTON was physically exhausted from everything that had happened, her mind continued to race.

She'd finally drifted to sleep, only to be awakened by horrible nightmares about everything. About being shot at. Being chased. The helicopter flying overhead.

But perhaps the biggest nightmare involved Rocco. His betrayal. The fact that he acted like he wanted to protect her all while he actually suspected her of being involved.

Afterward, she couldn't get back to sleep.

Instead, she turned over in bed. Every time she thought about Rocco's words, her heart panged.

When she finally glanced at the alarm clock on

her nightstand, the numbers there told her it was seven. Her body seemed programmed to wake up early. In actuality, she normally got up about five every morning so she could start things going at the bakery.

She pulled the blanket up tighter around her as she thought about her bakery with that broken window. Had looters come in and stolen anything? Were her customers wondering what had happened?

The fact that her shop was closed would certainly raise questions.

What about the police? Were they wondering if anything happened to her? Had they questioned anyone about her sudden disappearance?

Peyton should have called them. That definitely seemed clear now. Especially since she knew she'd been lured to that place under false circumstances.

And the only reason she was here was because Blackout wanted to keep her in their sights.

She turned over in bed as unease jostled inside her again.

Peyton had thought that she and Rocco shared a moment last night as they danced. She'd felt some sort of connection between them.

But, apparently, none of that was real either.

One thing became clear to her. Nobody else was going to fight to prove her innocence. Peyton was going to have to do that herself.

But exactly how would that work? How could she prove she was innocent while stuck here without any resources?

She could make phone calls, but she didn't know who to call other than her brother, who apparently knew nothing. She could call the police back in Norfolk and see if they would tell her anything. Yet that seemed doubtful also.

There had to be something she could do.

A knock sounded at her door.

Peyton jolted upright in bed.

Who was here? And why?

As much as she might want to avoid whoever was here or pretend she didn't hear, she knew that wouldn't be in her best interest. Instead she yelled, "Coming!"

Then she quickly tried to make herself more presentable.

It had to be Rocco.

Should she confront him about the conversation she'd overheard?

She nibbled on her bottom lip a moment.

No, she decided. She needed to play this cool.

Because she was much more likely to get answers if she did it that way.

ROCCO SMILED AS SOON as Peyton opened the door. Her hair was still messy from sleep, and she had no makeup on.

But she still looked beautiful.

He'd thought about her all night. Thought about the dance they shared. Thought about the way she'd smelled like vanilla and cinnamon.

Maybe Colton was right. Maybe it was time for Rocco to give love another chance.

"Good morning." He leaned in the doorway.

Peyton offered a quick smile. "Morning."

"I was wondering if you would like some breakfast."

She seemed to think about it for a moment before nodding. "I'm actually famished, now that you mention it."

Rocco was pleasantly surprised she'd said yes. "Great. Everyone's eating together down in the dining area. We'd love to have you join us."

Something flashed through Peyton's gaze, but it

quickly disappeared. "That sounds good. Give me a few minutes to freshen up, and then I'll be ready."

Rocco stepped inside the apartment and closed the door behind him as he waited.

A few minutes later, Peyton reappeared. Her hair was pulled back in a ponytail, and her eyes looked a little brighter.

She really was a sight to behold. A firecracker in her own way. Underestimated but strong. Happy but down-to-earth.

She paused beside him. As she did, Rocco felt something heat inside him. What was it about this woman that captured his attention so much?

He didn't know.

But maybe it would be wiser if he kept his distance—especially considering she might somehow be complicit in the events they were investigating.

CHAPTER TWENTY-EIGHT

PEYTON WANTED to be mad at Rocco. She *was* mad at him.

But why did the guy have to be so likable?

That was what really irritated her the most.

Still, it would do her no good to stay in her room alone. She needed to get some answers. The best way to do that was by being around these guys.

By listening. Observing. Asking the right questions.

As she and Rocco sat at a table with his friends, Peyton couldn't help but think that each of them seemed so much like good guys.

Maybe they *were* the good guys. Maybe they were the good guys and they thought *she* was the bad guy. Peyton frowned at the thought.

But she tried to act normal, to not let on what she knew.

After Rocco pushed away his empty plate, he cast a subtle grin at his teammates, a mischievous glimmer in his eyes.

"I bet you all the paperwork for this mission that it's another three months until we see Beckett smile."

The guys around the table laughed, Axel tapping Beckett on the back.

Rocco leaned toward Peyton. "Last time we saw him smile was eight months ago."

"Eight months?" she repeated, certain she hadn't heard correctly.

Beckett looked unfazed as he nodded, tapping his finger against his coffee mug. "I've been needing a good bet lately. I'm going to guess an average of six women will hit on Axel the next time we go out to eat together. If I'm right, you guys are doing my laundry for a whole week."

"We'll see about that." Axel shrugged, unbothered by the challenge as he dramatically brushed off his shoulders. "It's not like I'm trying to get them to hit on me. When you look as good as I do . . ."

The guys began hooting and hollering again.

"We know." Rocco raised his eyebrows and shook

his head. "We call that 'The Axel Way.' It's like he casts a magical spell on women wherever he goes."

"A magical spell is the only way I can explain why anyone would hit on this homely thing," Beckett muttered.

Axel chuckled and shook his head. "You're just jealous."

Despite herself, Peyton's curiosity rose. These guys certainly were interesting. Though she wasn't sure if she could trust them, she definitely wanted to know more about them.

"What about you?" She turned toward Rocco, unable to ignore her curiosity. "What kind of bets do people make about you?"

Before Rocco could answer, Axel spoke up. "We try to guess how many people will tell him how much they love his accent on any given day." He said the words with a fake British accent.

Rocco let out a deep chuckle. "You just keep casting your magic spells. I'll worry about the accent."

The rest of the conversation felt lighthearted—especially considering the circumstances. It was a welcome relief from Peyton's otherwise heavy thoughts.

But one other thing had confused Peyton. Axel

had mentioned Operation Grandiose and had blamed his bitter-tasting coffee on it. The rest of the guys had laughed, saying that everything was the fault of Operation Grandiose. What did that mean?

A few minutes later, after the rest of the crew left and it was just Peyton and Rocco, she decided to ask. After all, the more she knew about these guys, the easier it would be to find answers.

She gripped her coffee mug. "What was Axel talking about when he mentioned Operation Grandiose?"

As soon as Peyton asked the question, she realized that it was a mistake. The look on Rocco's face said it all.

His smile disappeared. His gaze darkened. His body stiffened.

But it was too late to take it back.

Maybe everything really was Operation Grandiose's fault.

THE NUMBER one thing Rocco didn't like talking about was Natalie. But the number two thing was Operation Grandiose.

But he believed in being open—when at all possible, at least.

He shifted in his seat, bracing himself to talk about the difficult subject. "Operation Grandiose was one of the last missions the guys and I were on together. It was after Natalie died and I'd gone back into the field."

Compassion filled Peyton's eyes as she waited for him to continue.

"Several of us from various SEAL teams were thrown together for the mission, which was in a remote area of Africa. Do you remember when I told you about having to stay awake for six days straight as insurgents tested us?"

Peyton nodded. "I do."

"That happened on this mission. We all thought we were going to die. To be truthful, none of us have been the same since then." Rocco swallowed hard, wishing his words weren't true. But they were.

"I'm sorry to hear that. Do you mean you haven't been the same mentally or physically?"

"A little bit of both." Rocco let out a long sigh. "It's strange the way we each came back from that mission with different ailments. But we all have something. I get migraines, for example. The insurgents sprayed something on us, and we wonder if that's what has affected us like this."

"That's terrible." Peyton frowned. "I'm really sorry to hear that."

"Two guys who were on that mission died recently." Rocco's throat burned as he said the words. It still didn't seem real. That loss would take time to process—time he didn't have right now.

Peyton's eyes widened. "Died? What do you mean?"

"I mean, in the same week, one man died in a car wreck and the other in a home invasion."

"In the same week?" Surprise laced her voice.

Rocco nodded somberly. "In the same week. We find that suspicious also."

"How many other people were on this mission?"

"There were nine of us all together. Beckett, Axel, Gabe, and I were there. The two men who died. And three other men."

"The other men . . . are they okay?"

"We called them and told them about what had happened. We weren't able to get up with one of the guys, though. Lucas Brandymere."

She frowned. "I'm sorry to hear that. I'm truly sorry for your loss. I can only imagine how hard that must be on you."

Peyton's soft, compassionate words loosened his muscles for a minute. She seemed to mean them.

Despite that, he was certain Peyton was hiding some kind of secret.

And the bigger question: was that secret deadly?

CHAPTER TWENTY-NINE

PEYTON CLEARED her throat before taking another sip of her coffee.

Her thoughts turned over in her mind.

Should she share with Rocco what she'd learned last night concerning Suzy? If she told Rocco, would she be playing into his plan? Would he somehow circle this back around and blame her—behind her back, of course?

She had no idea.

But Peyton didn't want to keep the news to herself anymore. In her gut, it didn't feel right to do so.

She leaned back in her chair at the dining table and glanced around. No one else was in the room except her and Rocco. The scent of bacon and sausage still rose around her, making this place feel like home.

It almost felt safe . . . but she had to remind herself it wasn't.

Appearances could be deceiving.

Like Rodger had been deceiving.

She'd gone through that situation with him . . . maybe it was to teach her to be more on guard. Like in this situation.

She set her mug back on the table. "I got a message from my brother last night. His assistant, the one who left that message for me . . ."

Rocco's gaze turned toward her, giving Peyton his full attention. "Suzy?"

"Yes, Suzy. She's missing. No one has heard from her since I got that message from her."

Rocco straightened, shifting in his seat. "You found out about this last night? You should have told me."

Peyton opened her mouth, tempted to tell him she'd tried. But then he might put it together that she'd overheard what he said. That wasn't what she wanted.

She shrugged instead. "I was tired, and I figured what was done was done."

Rocco stared at her another moment, and Peyton

willed her cheeks not to heat again. If they did, Rocco would be able to read her deception.

Finally, he nodded. "We'll look into it and see what we can find out."

"I'd appreciate it. Can I do anything to help? I know you guys are anxious to carry on with your other assignments, and I'm certainly anxious to get back to my life. Plus, I have clients to call and orders to cancel."

"I'm sorry for your change of plans, Peyton. I know you must feel like a tornado has ripped through your life."

When he said it like that—with his voice soft and his eyes so warm—Rocco sounded so sincere. He made her want to believe him. And that was dangerous.

She finally settled on saying, "I wish I knew who was doing this."

He leaned closer. "Have you thought of anybody else who might want to put you in the line of fire like this?"

Peyton licked her lips before finally saying, "The only person that I can think of would be my ex, Rodger. But I don't know that he'd go this far to make me suffer for breaking up with him."

"You said that he owned his own startup, right?"

"That's right. It's a doorbell company."

"A doorbell company?" A skeptical knot formed between his eyes.

"It's a smart doorbell," she explained, her words sounding lame. "The camera on it recognizes faces and sounds a different ring based on the person on the other side. That way, you know who's at the door."

"Branson's company deals with technology. It sounds like Rodger's company could fit right in."

As Rocco said the words, Peyton had to agree.

Maybe Rodger was the best bet after all.

Why hadn't she seen this earlier?

AFTER BREAKFAST, Rocco met with the rest of the guys for their morning debrief. He brought his cup of coffee with him as well as several questions that had been brewing in his mind.

He sat near the front of the table, near Colton.

"What's the latest on Quinn's and John's deaths?" Rocco asked after the meeting started.

"I put some feelers out to try to find more information, but I haven't heard anything yet." Colton stared at the iPad in his hands, the one listing everything on their agenda for the meeting.

"What about Lucas?" Axel asked. "Has anyone been able to get up with him yet?"

Lucas was another Navy SEAL who'd been on that mission with them. They'd already gotten up with Dave and Stephen.

"I'm back at square one," Colton said. "I tried to call last night and even once this morning. Lucas isn't answering his phone. I'm going to call his ex-girlfriend soon and see if she knows anything."

"Good idea." Rocco shifted in his seat. "I don't like what's happening."

"Neither do I. We'll keep looking into it, of course." Colton's jaw remained stiff as his gaze met each person's at the table. "In the meantime, I encourage everybody to watch their backs, just in case. Until we know what's going on, we need to be cautious."

"There's no doubt about that." Axel raised his eyebrows.

Colton leaned forward. "I just wanted to give everybody a brief rundown on everything that's going on. Branson will be leaving a little bit later today to head back to Norfolk. He doesn't want to make anyone suspicious with his appearance here."

"I'm surprised he came at all," Axel said.

"Branson is the type of guy who believes in looking people in the eye when he's talking to them," Colton said. "Says there's a lot that gets lost in translation when it comes to tech."

"That means a lot coming from a tech guy," Beckett muttered.

"That's true," Colton said. "We need to keep looking at who might be in on this in his company, but we're hoping that Gabe might provide us with more information. Especially if they plan to attempt another exchange. We don't want that to happen."

"I understand," Rocco said. "I just hate the fact that this technology is putting people's lives in danger. That's really why I want to get to the bottom of this. Peyton gave me the name of her old boyfriend, and I'm going to look into him to make sure he's not somehow involved with this."

He explained to them what Peyton's ex-boyfriend did.

"That sounds like a good idea," Colton said.

He divided up the rest of the tasks.

Rocco hoped they found some answers soon.

Because he could sense a storm on the horizon, and he wanted to do whatever he could to prevent it from destroying everything in its path.

CHAPTER THIRTY

THE LAST THING Peyton wanted to do was to sit in her room by herself. But she knew Rocco had a meeting.

Instead, she went down to the lobby, hoping at least to stretch her legs.

As she rounded the corner leading to an outside door, she stopped in her tracks. Bethany and Griff gave each other a lingering kiss goodbye.

Peyton quickly looked away, hating to interrupt the moment.

As Griff stepped outside, Bethany turned to her with a sheepish smile. "Sorry about that. But I won't see him for a few days and . . . you learn when you're married to someone with a high-stakes job to never take any time together for granted."

"How long have you been married?"

"Seven years. Give or take." Bethany shrugged.

"It's great that you guys can still look at each other like that." Peyton longed for that herself—to fall in love and stay in love. But that was one desire she needed to squelch. Love hadn't done right by her—and she doubted it ever would.

"What can I say? I still have a crush on him."

Peyton smiled. She liked the way Bethany had worded that. "A crush?"

"I figure as long as I have a crush on my husband, I know things are good between us. He's infuriating sometimes, but I wouldn't trade him for the world." Bethany rested her hand on her belly.

Peyton's gaze lingered there for a moment before she looked away, trying not to stare.

"We are expecting another baby in about six months," Bethany explained.

"Congratulations. That's great."

Her cheeks flushed. "Thank you. We're really excited too. Before too long, this whole campus will be filled with kids. Ada will be thrilled."

"I take it others are expecting babies also?"

She nodded. "That's right. Elise—she's Colton's wife—is expecting about a month after me. The police chief here in town—her husband helped to start Blackout—she's also expecting. We're so excited."

Peyton's heart panged with a feeling she hadn't expected. She thought at this point in her life she'd be baking cakes for her own child's birthday party. But that hadn't happened. Still, she couldn't complain. Most days, at least, she was doing what she loved to earn her living.

But that didn't mean she didn't feel a little emptiness inside her sometimes.

"Listen, I've got to run pick up Ada from CJ's place. But I'd love to chat with you again sometime. Your cupcakes were phenomenal last night. Thank you again so much for making those for Ada."

Peyton grinned. "It was no problem. I'm glad you enjoyed them."

As Bethany hurried away, Peyton's phone buzzed.

The number was unknown.

She glanced at the text message anyway.

Actually, it wasn't a text message.

It was a video.

Her finger hovered above the Play button as she contemplated whether or not it was wise to watch whatever had been sent.

PEYTON'S EX-BOYFRIEND was everything Rocco had assumed he would be. Arrogant. Stuck on himself. Narcissistic.

Dger.

Rocco shook his head. The outrageous nickname seemed appropriate for someone with an ego as big as his.

As much as Rocco wanted to pin what was happening on somebody like Dger, he couldn't find anything in the man's past that indicated he was guilty of these things.

The man's startup *did* involve tech. But this guy didn't seem to be as much about power as he did attention and control. His product was still a prototype, and he was trying to raise enough funding to get it off the ground.

Rocco sat at his desk and took another sip of his coffee.

Whoever was behind this whole fiasco clearly had resources. They'd hired gunmen to come and destroy the scene where the exchange was supposed to take place. They also hired someone in that helicopter to come after Rocco and Peyton.

He could only assume that Peyton was the target here and not him.

His mind again went back to that video of Peyton throwing the brick at her bakery.

He wanted to ask her about it. He wanted to see her face when she tried to explain whatever it was that had happened. If he hadn't seen that video with his own eyes, he wouldn't have believed it.

Out of curiosity, Rocco ran another background check on her brother. Anderson did work in finance. He'd started his own company and appeared to be doing pretty well for himself.

Someone had clearly used Anderson's name to lure Peyton to the scene the night of the exchange. They'd also pulled in his secretary, Suzy, who was now missing. Then there was the fact that Karen, Peyton's best friend, had been killed that same day.

No matter which way Rocco looked at this, it didn't make sense. It was like various parts of random pieces of equipment had been laid out, and now someone was asking Rocco's team to make a machine out of them. The task seemed impossible, however.

He picked up the phone and texted Gabe, anxious to hear if he'd learned anything yet. He asked him to give him a call when he had a minute.

To Rocco's surprise, his phone rang a moment later. It was Gabe.

"How's it going?" Rocco asked.

"Good, I guess. I mean, I haven't discovered anything yet. I've just met a lot of people. I have a lot of names floating around in my head. This is going to take time, and I know we don't have time."

"I know. This is a long game. Just keep your eyes open for anyone suspicious. If we can figure out who's trying to sell this information from the company, that would be a great starting place for figuring out everything else that's happened."

"I'm hoping to dig in more deeply starting tomorrow. Is that why you wanted me to call? Because I already talked to Colton about this."

"I'm actually calling because somebody in relation to this case is missing. Someone named Suzy Belmont. She's the administrative assistant to Anderson Ellison, Peyton's brother. Suzy disappeared, and we're trying to figure out if she had anything to do with what's going on."

"Do you want me to look into it?"

"That would be great. Since you're already up in Norfolk, you'll have the best opportunity to learn what happened to her. As soon as we end the call, I'll send you her information, including her address."

"Sounds like a plan. Send it my way. I'll see what I can find out."

"Thanks, Gabe. And be careful."

"You know it."

You know it? That was another of Gabe's classic sayings.

Just like Axel always said, "And that's how it all went down."

Rocco supposed what he liked most about his team was that they all had unique and vastly different personalities.

Rocco was curious about how this was all going to go down. He hoped they could find some answers before tragedy struck again.

CHAPTER THIRTY-ONE

PEYTON'S EYES widened as she watched the video for the third time.

The first time, she hadn't been sure what she had seen.

The second time, she'd struggled to know if what she was seeing was correct.

The third time, she wanted confirmation.

Yet she didn't.

She wanted to pretend that she had never seen this.

But these images would never be erased from her mind.

Rocco and his team might make themselves out to be noble guardians of America. But, in truth, there was nothing noble about them, was there?

The video was grainy, but Rocco, Beckett, Axel, and Gabe's faces were all clear.

They were wearing military garb. Carrying big guns. And they appeared to be in what looked like a battlefield.

Peyton couldn't make out any of the audio. But the video seemed to have come from a camera, possibly on someone's helmet.

She watched as Rocco took a gas can and poured liquid from it all around the building. His teammates helped him.

When they were done, Rocco led them away before setting the building on fire.

Peyton watched in horror as a woman inside ran to the window screaming for help.

But instead of helping her, the team simply watched.

Almost as if they didn't hear her.

How could somebody consider themselves noble while doing something like that?

It didn't matter to Peyton how honorable these guys thought themselves to be. All she cared about was the fact that she now knew just how despicable they really were.

Everything that she had thought about them was incorrect. These guys were not on the side of justice.

They were the bad guys.

And she was stuck here at this facility with them.

With no car.

But she did have a cell phone, she remembered.

Maybe she could call for help. Get away from here.

The last time she tried that, someone had chased her.

Exactly whom could she trust right now?

It wasn't a question Peyton ever thought she would have to ask herself. At least, not in a situation like this.

She leaned her head back against her bed as her temples began to pound.

It was no longer enough for her just to stay here until this blew over.

She was going to have to be proactive and figure out her next step.

Because the only person she had to watch out for herself was . . . herself.

"I TALKED to one of Suzy's friends," Gabe told Rocco three hours later.

Rocco sat in his office, fighting off a headache

again. Hearing an encouraging update from Gabe just might be what he needed to get rid of his migraine for good.

"And?" Rocco asked.

"She said Suzy packed her bags and left to go out of town. She didn't really give any reason for it. Her friend didn't even think to ask about it either."

Rocco tapped his pen against the table. "So her friend didn't think it was suspicious?"

"She thought it was a little weird, but she said Suzy's been acting strangely lately."

"Any idea why?"

"Here's where it gets interesting," Gabe's voice lilted. "Her friend said she started dating somebody new, and ever since then she's been acting more secretive."

"Does her friend have any idea who Suzy is dating?"

"She doesn't know anything for certain, but she's pretty sure Suzy is dating her boss."

"Anderson Ellison?"

"The one and only. But apparently, Suzy doesn't believe in workplace romances, especially not with her boss. She thinks that's why Suzy was acting so cagey lately. She didn't want anyone to find out."

Anderson's name had come up again. Rocco wondered if he was somehow connected to all this.

That's what Rocco was more inclined to think all the time.

Rocco thanked Gabe for the update, ended the call, and then stood. He needed to talk to Peyton. Maybe she had some answers, but she just didn't know it.

He stretched before walking up to her room and knocking on the door.

But when she answered, the perky Peyton he'd become accustomed to didn't answer.

Instead, her eyes looked accusatory. Maybe even angry.

Rocco braced himself.

Because he sensed something was wrong.

Really wrong.

CHAPTER THIRTY-TWO

PEYTON FELT outrage wash through her again when she saw Rocco standing in the hallway outside her door. She couldn't pretend she hadn't seen that video. Like she didn't know the truth.

But she didn't know the best way to handle this yet either.

She had to plan her next move—if she wanted to live, at least.

"Peyton." Rocco nodded at her, but the action seemed stiffer than usual, almost like he sensed she'd discovered who he truly was.

She crossed her arms. "Rocco."

He tilted his head. "Can I come in?"

She thought about it for a moment before

backing up and allowing him inside. But she refused to break from her icy disposition.

He paused just inside the doorway. "Is everything okay?"

She closed the door and shook her head. "As a matter of fact, no. It's not okay."

His hands went to his hips as he waited for her to continue. "What happened?"

She thought about it another moment. Pretend like she didn't know? Or confront this head on?

She usually took the non-conflict way out.

But that hadn't gotten her very far in life.

Besides, holding this in would only cause her hard feelings to fester.

She held up her phone and hit Play on the video. "This is what happened. All this time, you guys made yourselves out to be these white knights who ride in to save the day. Men who put their lives on the line for the betterment of our country. But, in truth, you guys have no morals at all."

"Peyton—"

"I'm not saying that to sound judgmental. I know that sometimes bad things have to happen in order for good to prevail, and I'm not here to argue the ethics of that. But there's no way I can watch this video of you guys burning a woman's house with her inside—"

"What?" Surprise echoed in his voice.

Before Peyton offered, Rocco took the phone from her and stared at the screen.

She watched as his eyes narrowed and his shoulders stiffened.

His gaze flickered up to hers, his entire being seeming to go still. "Where did you get this?"

Interesting that the first thing he didn't do was to deny it. That's what Peyton would do in a situation like that.

"Someone sent it to me."

"Who?" he demanded.

"It was an unknown number, if you must know."

He looked up at her again and shook his head. "This isn't what you think it is."

"I don't know what else it could be other than you guys killing an innocent woman."

"You don't understand . . . this isn't us."

"Clearly, it is. I can see your faces. It's one thing if somebody shares secondhand knowledge. But if I can see proof with my own eyes—"

Rocco stepped toward her, and his voice dipped lower. "Peyton, you've got to believe me. This isn't us."

Believe him?

That was what always got her in trouble.

ROCCO STILL COULDN'T BELIEVE the images he'd seen.

The video footage looked incredibly real. Rocco had to watch it again himself. What he saw and what he knew clashed with each other.

He understood why Peyton was upset. The recording looked authentic.

Then he remembered the video of Peyton throwing that brick, and facts began to click together in his mind.

"I think we need to sit down," he said.

"I'm not sure I want to sit down with you," Peyton said. "This whole time, you've been deceiving me."

"I really need to explain something to you," Rocco said. "I know you're upset. But I think things will make more sense once we talk."

She still raised her chin in that stubborn, determined manner. "I'm just not sure that's a good idea. I need to call somebody and get away from this place.

I don't know where I'm going to go or what I'm going to do but—"

Rocco stepped forward and squeezed her arm, knowing he was taking a risk and she might slug him across the jaw. He only knew he needed to try to get through to her.

"Give me five minutes of your time. That's all I need. And after I explain, if you still want to call somebody and take off, feel free. I'll even help you get away from Blackout. But there's something that you need to know."

Peyton stared at him a moment before stiffly lowering herself onto the couch.

Rocco started to sit beside her but changed his mind and took a chair on the other side of the coffee table instead.

"One minute." He pulled out his phone and looked through the messages until he found the video of Peyton.

Rocco pressed Play before handing it to her. He watched Peyton's expression as she watched the video. Surprise. Shock. Outrage.

She swung her head back and forth as she looked up at him. Her lips parted and a fire lit in her gaze.

"I did *not* break the window to my bakery. Why would I even do that?"

"The video makes it look like you did."

"I *know* what the video looks like, but I was there. Or I *wasn't* there, I should say. I don't even know what I'm trying to say except that I didn't do this. That's not me." She threw her hands in the air, her curls flying along with the motion.

He stood and moved closer, sat next to her on the couch. "Then where did this video come from? And how did it get in this business's security feed?"

She squinted at the screen as if trying to get a better look.

"I'd like to say that somebody was imitating me. But that woman looks just like me. It doesn't make any sense." She paused and sucked in a breath. Her wide eyes climbed up until they met Rocco's. "That's not you in that video either, is it?"

Rocco shook his head, glad she'd seen his point finally. "It isn't."

She fell back into the couch, almost looking exhausted. Definitely perplexed. Maybe even dumbfounded.

"What's going on here, Rocco?"

"That's what we need to figure out. I've been

sitting on this video of you, wondering if I could trust you also."

Questions saturated her gaze as she looked up at him. "Somebody wants to turn us against each other."

"Someone's definitely playing some type of sick game."

She closed her eyes and rubbed her forehead. "I thought I was confused before, but now I'm *really* confused. I don't even know who or what to trust."

"I want you to know that you can trust me. I know it's hard. That you hardly know me at all. But I'm not lying to you."

Her eyes flicked open, and her gaze locked with his. "I haven't lied to you either. But . . . how did someone even do this?"

"Have you ever put videos of yourself online?"

She shrugged. "Sure. I've been in some televised bake-off competitions. I did an online cooking show for a while, just on a YouTube channel. But there's plenty of video footage of me out there if somebody looks hard enough."

Rocco nodded slowly. "I think that's how this happened. I think that somebody pulled some of that footage and spliced it together to make it look like this."

"What about the video footage of you? How did they do that?"

He let out a heavy sigh. "There are training videos of my guys. That's my best guess. But what I'm unsure about is how somebody might have gotten their hands on something like that."

"Nothing online is secure anymore, is it?"

"You're right. It doesn't matter what type of firewalls are put up. There always seems to be somebody who's capable of breaking through them."

Peyton stared at him, her chin quivering for a minute. "I have to admit, the thought of all this terrifies me. If someone can make it look like I broke the window to my bakery, what else can they make me look guilty of? Or you?"

The questions hung in the air.

That was exactly what Rocco had been thinking also.

CHAPTER THIRTY-THREE

ROCCO WAS STILL TRYING to process everything he'd just learned.

Those videos were a lot to swallow—especially since they weren't real.

That's what made them even scarier.

He shifted closer to Peyton. She was still visibly shaken—as anyone would be in this situation. That video had truly shocked her.

Just as the video of Rocco's team had shocked him.

When you couldn't trust what you saw with your own eyes, then what could you trust?

That was the question lingering in his mind.

"We're going to get to the bottom of this," he assured her.

"I wish I felt that confident."

Rocco placed his hand on her back, wishing he could calm her. He hated to see her so upset. "Just trust me."

Her wavering gaze met his. "Trust is something that's hard if you don't know what to believe."

He stared deeply into her eyes. "What does your gut tell you? Do your instincts tell you that you can trust me?"

Peyton looked up at him a moment, and he was almost afraid that she was going to say no. But finally, she nodded. "They do."

He reached forward and pushed a hair behind her ear. "I like you, Peyton. I really do. I don't want to see anything happen to you. But my guys and I are going to need some time to sort this out."

"Of course."

"I need you to stay in here while I go share this update. As soon as I can, I'll come and tell you if we have learned anything. But the best thing that you can do right now is stay here where I will know you're safe."

Emotions swirled in her gaze as she lifted her head toward him.

Rocco wished he'd known her longer. Or that he knew her better. Because he had the strange urge to reach over and give her a lingering kiss to show her everything was going to be okay.

But this wasn't the time or the place.

He hoped he might get to do something like that later.

The realization surprised even him. He'd had walls up around his heart for a long time—since Natalie. The idea of letting them down left Rocco feeling raw and exposed. As a SEAL, those were two feelings he didn't embrace.

"I'll stay here." Peyton said the words so softly he'd hardly heard her.

Rocco nodded and pulled his hand back.

He'd stay here with her longer if he could. But he couldn't.

Too much was on the line. Too much that he had to do.

Rocco had a feeling that this all somehow went back to that technology that Branson was trying to sell. But a feeling wasn't enough to prove anything.

Then again, neither was a video.

And that was going to make finding answers even more difficult.

PEYTON LEANED BACK on the couch after Rocco left.

Was it just her or was something going on between the two of them? That's definitely how it felt.

There was a spark. A connection. A... hope?

But that idea seemed crazy, especially given the circumstances. It must be the danger that was making all of Peyton's senses feel more heightened. She was vulnerable. Alone. Scared.

That was the perfect time to fall for someone, right?

But what if it wasn't? Or what if it wasn't just that?

Peyton didn't know, but she could still feel the warmth of Rocco's hand from where it had rested on her back. If she closed her eyes, she could visualize the warm look in his eyes—a look that said he was open to being more than friends once all this was over.

He'd said he liked her, hadn't he?

The memory heated her cheeks.

Because she knew she liked him too.

Peyton believed him when he told her it wasn't him in the video. Because she knew that wasn't her in the video he'd shown her.

What kind of twisted scheme was going on here?

She didn't know, but somehow, she found herself in the middle of it, and she wanted to help Rocco and his guys get to the bottom of this.

But she couldn't. Not now.

She needed to stay here. That was what Rocco had asked her to do. The last thing she needed to do was to give him one more thing to worry about.

Because, really, he had a lot of information to uncover. But maybe now that they had discovered those altered videos, that would give him a good place to start.

CHAPTER THIRTY-FOUR

"WHO WOULD HAVE access to video footage like this?" Rocco glanced around the table at the members of his team.

"That's a great question," Colton said. "But I have to admit that anybody with any type of good hacking skills could have probably accessed it from a military server."

"It would have to be somebody on the inside," Beckett said. "There are too many firewalls in place for just anybody to get through."

"But we were deliberately set up," Axel said. "Somebody wants to scare us with this footage. Because if it goes public . . ."

He didn't have to finish his statement. They all knew where he was going with it.

A lot of damage could be done.

The video played again on a screen in the background, and they all stared at it.

"It looks so real . . ." Beckett ran a hand over his face. "I just can't believe it."

"I mean if I wasn't there, I would think that that was us," Axel said.

"And that's exactly what Peyton said about that video of her throwing the brick into her bakery window," Rocco said.

"So maybe she really has been a victim this whole time," Axel said.

"That's my best guess. Somebody is playing mind games with us."

"Whoever is behind this is deep into the tech world," Colton said. "They're able to manipulate footage. And I have a feeling that we've had some sort of Big Brother watching over us lately."

Rocco turned his gaze toward his leader, wondering what he was getting at. "What do you mean?"

"I mean, someone has known our every move. They knew when Peyton left. They knew when she was riding down the road with you driving the car. They knew we brought her back here."

"And how are they watching us? Are they controlling satellites in the sky?" The way Beckett worded the question made it clear that he was skeptical.

"It doesn't have to be that extreme," Colton said. "They could have figured out a way to hack into our security cameras themselves. They could access the GPS data on our vehicles or on our phones. They could access other security camera footage to keep an eye on us. Technology can be wonderful. But it can also be dangerous."

"Didn't somebody use that very technology to stage a drone attack here last year?" Beckett asked.

Colton frowned and nodded. "As a matter of fact, they did. And we're all lucky to be alive after that happened."

"So, if this is true, then whoever is behind this is hiding behind a computer. How do we even find somebody like that?" Axel asked.

"That's a great question," Colton said. "Anybody have any ideas?"

PEYTON COULDN'T BELIEVE everything that had happened. Her mind was still reeling every time she thought about that video of her throwing a brick through the window at the bakery.

It looked so real.

Somebody had wanted Rocco and the rest of the Blackout guys to believe she was involved here. That she was a player in this deadly game. That she was only pretending to be innocent and clueless.

Peyton's hands fisted at her side as anger swelled in her.

Why would someone want to make her look guilty? She could understand if she were involved with some shady business dealings and somebody wanted to frame her. But she wasn't.

So why?

Rodger's face appeared in her mind.

Had Rocco looked into him? Yet, this wasn't the kind of crime Peyton could see her ex being involved with.

Who did that leave? Who did she know that might kill Karen or make Suzy disappear?

Her brother?

Peyton shook her head. She couldn't believe that. She *wouldn't* believe it.

She and her brother had always had each other's backs. Ever since their parents had essentially walked out of their lives, it had just been the two of them. Her brother would never have done this to her.

She crossed his name off her mental list.

So who else?

Peyton let out a sigh.

She had no idea, and that was what made this all the more baffling.

As her thoughts went back to Rocco, a small smile began to curl her lips.

She hadn't been excited about the possibility of dating someone in a long, long time. But something was different about Rocco. She could really see herself falling for him.

He was kind. Honest. He didn't scoff when she acted silly or put her down when she messed up.

Plus, he was handsome to boot. Really, really handsome.

Whenever Peyton heard that accent . . . she felt like she could listen to him talk all day.

Just then, her phone buzzed, and she glanced at the screen.

It was Rocco.

Did he have an update?

Peyton hoped so.

"Hey," she answered, trying to make her voice sound not quite as breathless as she felt.

"Hey, Peyton. Listen, I discovered something that you're going to want to know."

"What is it?" She sat up straighter, anxious to hear the update.

"I can't tell you now, and I can't tell you on the phone. Can you meet me by the gate?"

"You want to go off campus?" Peyton needed to make sure that she understood his unusual request correctly.

"I have to make sure that nobody else is around to listen. I'll have my car waiting for you. Then we can talk."

She hesitated for a moment. But this was clearly Rocco she was talking to. His accent and tone were unmistakable.

Then why did she feel a surge of alarm?

"I'll be there in five minutes," she murmured.

"Good. I'll see you then. Try not to let anyone see you leave. I don't want to raise anybody's suspicions."

The tension inside her threaded more tightly.

She didn't know what was going on, but she was anxious to find out.

CHAPTER THIRTY-FIVE

"THAT'S GOT TO BE IT," Rocco said. "Branson wasn't being honest with us. This technology that he's been developing . . . it's dangerous. No wonder terrorists have been anxious to get their hands on it."

"It's called deep fakes." Colton shook his head, his eyes narrowed with tension. "It's when people can change the media and make it appear real."

"Kind of like that video that came out about us?" Axel asked.

"Exactly like that. That kind of technology is dangerous. Very dangerous."

"So what do we do about it now?" Beckett asked.

"We need evidence," Rocco said.

"How are you going to find that?" Axel asked.

"It's hard to find evidence when so much of it can be manufactured to fit a narrative. I've heard of some AI programs that are on the brink of being amazing and game-changing. But this stuff . . . it's so high-quality that you can't tell the real thing from the fabricated."

"I know, and that's what makes it scary."

They sat silently for a minute.

Once they started doubting something, it was easy to doubt everything. Any type of evidence that you may have been sent. Messages. Texts. Videos.

All that could be fabricated.

And the thought was absolutely terrifying on more than one level.

With technology like this somebody could manufacture the president or other high-ranking political or military figures saying or doing things that weren't true. And in the court of public opinion, they would be crucified.

Skills like that in the hands of the wrong person could end up being deadly. They could cause wars. From inside the country and from outside, this was some serious stuff.

"I need to talk to Peyton again," Rocco said. "She's connected with this somehow. Maybe we just haven't dug deep enough."

"Maybe. Take ten minutes and then meet me back here again," Colton said. "We have to figure this out. And from now on, all our communication needs to be face-to-face. Whoever is behind this clearly knows what he's doing. We can't chance someone trying to pull the wool over our eyes."

The bad feeling that had been brewing in Rocco's gut continued to ferment as he walked to Peyton's room. Once there, he knocked at the door but there was no answer.

Strange.

When he'd left her, he'd felt confident that she would remain in the room where she would be safe. Especially in light of everything that had been shared.

So why wasn't she answering?

He knew the campus was secure. After a breach not long ago, they had doubled up on all their security here. Nobody was getting in and out of this place without clearance.

He found his key card and unlocked the door, praying that she was simply in the shower or sleeping.

But he had a feeling that wasn't the case.

He stepped inside. "Peyton?"

No answer.

He stepped deeper into the space. "Peyton?"

Still no answer.

He looked around the rest of the small apartment.

She was gone.

But where?

And had she gone willingly or had somebody somehow managed to take her?

PEYTON SLIPPED out of the door of the Daniel Oliver Building and glanced around. It was dark outside.

But the darkness would be her friend right now.

Rocco had said not to let anybody see her leaving. And if he said that, he must have a good reason for it.

She shivered at the thought of what she might be about to find out. She didn't want to be frightened, but she was. She'd never been in dangerous situations like this before all this started.

But now here she was. Again.

But she had to keep her eyes on the goal of getting out of this situation alive.

She hurried down the gravel lane, keeping to the

edge of it where the shadows were darker. As she glanced around, she didn't see anybody else out there.

She picked up her pace when she saw the black vehicle waiting on the other side of the guard station.

Rocco really didn't want anybody else to see them meeting, did he?

Does that mean he found out information about somebody who was on the inside? It was the only thing that made sense. And now he wanted to get her away from this place before the wrong person found out.

She didn't like the sound of this.

A few minutes later, she reached the guard station. She pressed her palm onto the button that would release the gate.

It opened entirely too slowly, swinging out like it had all the time in the world.

As soon as possible, she squeezed between it and darted toward the dark SUV waiting there.

As she approached it, the back door opened.

The back door?

Rocco must have brought somebody else into this. Colton? Beckett?

She was about to find out.

She gave one last glance at the Blackout building before diving into the car.

But the person she saw inside wasn't who she expected.

CHAPTER THIRTY-SIX

"THERE SHE IS." Colton pointed to the TV screen inside the guard station. "She climbed into this black SUV about ten minutes ago."

Rocco's jaw clenched as he stepped back from the security footage that showed Peyton leaving the Blackout campus.

Why in the world had Peyton gotten into that vehicle? It made no sense—especially after all they'd talked about.

"She's in trouble," Rocco said. "We've got to find her."

"The ferries aren't running right now," Colton said. "That means she has to be on this island—unless somebody was crazy enough to leave with her by boat at this time of night."

"Let's hope that's not it. We need to find her."

"Get everybody together and get moving," Colton said.

"I'll call Cassidy. We've got to let everybody know that whoever is behind this is good. Really good. At this point, I'm not even sure that I trust that I'm talking to the right person on the other end of a phone line."

Colton rubbed his neck. "You're right. We're going to have to be very careful what our next steps are. Remember, if you're not communicating face-to-face, be extra cautious."

"Will do," Rocco said. "I don't want to waste any more time. I'm going to head out."

"Okay but be careful."

"I will." Rocco started outside toward his vehicle.

He wished he had a way to get in contact with Peyton. But he'd found her phone in her apartment. When he'd looked at her call list, it showed Peyton had received a phone call from him—only he hadn't called her.

Anger burned through his blood at the thought of it. Somebody was playing a twisted game right now.

But he was going to find Peyton if it was the last thing that he did.

In the meantime, he'd search every inch of this island.

She had to be here somewhere.

And he was going to find her.

PEYTON BACKED up against the door, reaching for the handle.

The man beside her let out a *tsk tsk*. "I wouldn't do that if I were you."

When she looked down, she saw the gun casually perched in his hands.

Her gaze flung back up to meet the man's. He scrutinized her with his beady eyes as he propped a cowboy-boot-clad leg across his knee.

"Who are you?" The words sounded raw as they left her lips.

"You'll see." The man smirked.

Peyton studied his face, trying to figure out if he looked familiar.

That's when the truth hit her.

"You're Branson Tartus . . ." The words left her lips as something close to a whisper.

His smirk diminished. "It's not important who I am."

Questions raced through her mind so quickly that she felt lightheaded. "I just don't understand. What do you want with me?"

"You really don't know yet, do you?"

"No, I have no idea. I have absolutely nothing to offer you. I think you're smart enough to know that."

"Well, I guess you're just going to have to wait to find out then. In the meantime, don't make any sudden moves. Because I'm not going to shoot to kill. But I could make your life very difficult until I get what I want from you."

Peyton felt herself shrinking as she pressed herself into the corner, trying to get as far away from the man as she could.

But what about that call from Rocco?

At once, the realization hit her.

If these guys could create videos that seemed realistic, no doubt they could also take somebody's voice and manipulate it to say things that hadn't actually been said. That was what that phone call to her had been about, hadn't it?

A sickly feeling began to drip into her already acidic stomach.

Peyton had to figure out what she was going to do.

Because if she didn't have a plan, then there was a good chance that she was about to die.

CHAPTER THIRTY-SEVEN

WHO WAS IN THAT CAR?

That was the question that kept repeating itself over and over again in Rocco's mind as the team reconvened in the conference room.

The person inside must be the one who'd orchestrated all this. The fake videos. The fake phone calls. The fake setup.

Rocco still wasn't 100 percent sure what this person's motives were. But he was getting close. So close.

He could feel it in his bones.

He'd already looked into Rodger. But Rodger had a clear alibi. He had been posting pictures on his social media of himself in the Caribbean all week. Plus, the man seemed too shallow to pull something like this off. If anything, he would be a player in this kind of scheme. But not the person calling the shots.

The person in charge was smart. Maybe even too smart for his own good.

"I called Gabe," Axel announced. "He said Branson isn't back at work yet. He also said people have been eyeing him all day."

"Eyeing him?" Colton repeated.

"Like they're suspicious of him," Axel said.

Rocco shifted. "Has he been made?"

"That's his feeling."

"He should get out of there the first chance he can," Colton said.

"That's what I told him too." Axel nodded affirmatively.

"I say we go pay Branson a visit ourselves," Rocco said. "See if he's still on the island after all."

Colton stood. "I think that's a great idea."

Did Branson have Peyton? Was he the one who'd set her up to take the fall for this? Was he the one who had hired Blackout—but only so they could look like the bad guys when all of this was over?

Rocco wasn't sure. But he needed to see things for himself before he would believe anything again.

"WHERE ARE WE?" Peyton glanced at the house in the distance. It was two stories and up on stilts, like most in the area were. There was nothing remarkable or flashy about the outside.

"You'll see soon enough."

Branson kept a tight grip on her arm as he shoved her up the steps.

The guy who had been driving the car rushed past them. He unlocked the front door and threw it open.

Branson thrust Peyton inside.

She caught her balance just in time to stop in her tracks.

"Anderson?" she gaped.

She stared at her brother.

He was tied up to a chair on the other side of the room. One eye was black, and his lip was busted. Blood streaked his shirt, and his hair was disheveled.

What had these men done to him?

"Isn't this a happy reunion?" Branson closed and locked the door behind him before stepping closer, acting coolly in control as his cowboy boots echoed across the wood floor.

The shades inside were all drawn, the only light flickering from an outdated overhead fixture.

"Why do you have my brother?" Peyton stared at Branson, desperate for things to make sense.

"Why don't you tell her?" Branson glanced at her brother, an unknown emotion flashing in his gaze.

Anderson shook his head, which was still lowered, almost as if he didn't have the strength to raise it. "I'm sorry, Peyton. I never meant for things to get out of control like this."

Fear froze her insides, spreading its icy fingers until she could hardly breathe. "What are you talking about?"

Anderson remained quiet, his gaze haggard as he stared at her. Despair lined his eyes—despair and exhaustion.

"Tell her." Branson raised his gun and shoved it into Peyton's ribcage hard enough that she let out a whimper.

Peyton tried to back away. But she couldn't.

Branson was on one side of her and his driver/bodyguard on the other.

"Anderson?" She stared at her brother, waiting expectantly for an answer.

"None of this was supposed to happen," he rushed. "You were never supposed to be involved."

Realization hit her. Her brother was somehow part of this.

Her heart crashed into her stomach at the thought of it.

"What did you do?" Her voice came out sounding breathless as she stared at him.

Anderson shook his head. "One of my friends works at the company and told me what they were developing. I wanted to invest in that kind of groundbreaking technology, but Branson here didn't want me to. He'd rather sell that kind of information to the terrorists so they can use it."

"No, you've got it wrong." Peyton swung her head back and forth. "Terrorists are trying to steal the information from him. One of his employees betrayed him."

Anderson stared at her, something unspoken in his gaze.

That's when Peyton realized the truth.

She glanced at the man beside her—the bodyguard.

He wore all black with a baseball cap pulled down low over his eyes.

He was the man who'd been out there that night when Peyton had delivered her cupcakes.

"Who set up that meeting?" Peyton shook her head, not wanting to believe what she knew was true. "Why pretend somebody else is trying to buy this?"

"So Branson doesn't get arrested," Anderson said. "If the wrong people get their hands on this technology, it will be a game changer. The deep fakes Branson is able to create can trick anybody. If there's a political candidate you don't like? Create video footage proving he did something wrong. If there's a social justice movement you want to take on? Stage fake phone calls with those involved that will make people question everything they know."

"And you wanted to be a part of that?" Peyton stared at her brother again.

"I didn't want to be on the wrong side of it." Sweat covered Anderson's upper lip now. "This could also be used for a lot of good. But Branson didn't let me even have a chance to help him out."

"I didn't need his help," Branson growled.

"So you set up that meeting so my brother would be caught?" Peyton still tried to put the pieces together.

"I set up that meeting to involve you." Branson squeezed her arm harder. "I knew if I had you in my crosshairs that your brother would do whatever I wanted. However, I didn't expect the Blackout guys to save you."

"But you hired them." He wasn't making any sense. Then again, Peyton couldn't pretend to think like someone this twisted did. Still, the man was intelligent. He'd obviously put some thought into this.

"I set everything up. I even planted that burner phone with the fake message on it to make it seem like one of my employees was involved. Blackout was supposed to take the fall for killing you," Branson said. "But instead, they saved you and got away."

"And you've just been playing games ever since?" Peyton still couldn't believe any of this. It seemed surreal.

"That's right." Branson smiled—not a friendly smile. It was dark and twisted. "And I'm not done yet. You all have been the perfect practice for all the tech I've been developing and the various ways it can be used."

CHAPTER THIRTY-EIGHT

"ANDERSON ELLISON HAS GONE OFF GRID." Axel walked back into the conference room, excitement lighting his gaze. "Nobody has seen him in at least three days."

"He was supposed to be in Detroit." Rocco remembered the phone call Peyton had made to her brother when they'd first picked her up.

"He wasn't." Axel shook his head. "I called several people to confirm that."

Before they could ask any more questions, the door opened and Beckett strode inside. "Branson isn't at his rental house, and his car is gone. Any idea what kind of vehicle he was driving?"

"It was parked around the back of the building when I dropped him off yesterday," Rocco said. "I didn't get a good look at it, but how much do you want to bet it was a black SUV?"

Colton crossed his arms, a pensive expression on his face. "If that's true, how does Anderson tie in with this?"

"Maybe the two of them are working together," Axel suggested.

"I have more information." Beckett scowled as if annoyed that he'd been interrupted. "I went into The Crazy Chefette and showed Anderson's picture around. That new waitress who just started working there—Olivia, I think her name is. She said she recognized him. Said he came in last night."

Rocco bristled at the update. "So Anderson Ellison is on the island as well as Branson Tartus? The question is, where are they now? Because if we can find them, I bet we'll find Peyton."

Axel went to the computer and typed in several things before muttering, "Apparently, Anderson isn't as smart as he thinks he is."

Rocco stood behind him. "What are you talking about?"

"I just pinged his cell phone number. His last known location? Lantern Beach."

Colton straightened. "Do you have an address?"

Axel hit another key and nodded. "I sure do."

Rocco stepped toward the door. "Then let's get geared up and head out. There's no time to waste."

"I'll call Cassidy and let her know what's going on." Beckett pulled his phone out as they started toward the door.

Rocco's throat tightened.

They had to get to Peyton.

He only hoped that it wasn't too late.

PEYTON FELT the tremble rake through her. "What are you planning on doing with me?"

Branson shoved the gun deeper into her ribcage.

Then he turned his beady gaze on Anderson. "You're going to make a video and confess that everything was your fault. If you don't, then your sister is going to die here right in front of your eyes."

"You're going through all this trouble just to make my brother look guilty?" Peyton didn't bother to hide the disgust in her voice.

"I would use my technology to fake his video confession, but there simply isn't enough time for that." Branson narrowed his gaze at her brother. "Anderson here is going to be the one who looks guilty for selling this technology to terrorists—and possibly for killing his sister after she got in the way of his greedy little plan."

"Seems like a lot of trouble to go through for a paltry payoff," Peyton muttered, still staring at her brother as if doing so would give her more answers.

"My plan has been ever evolving. But each step, each revision gave me a chance to test out all my technology." A certain smugness entered Branson's voice.

"You mean the fake videos? The fake phone calls? The fake news articles even?" More disgust dripped in her stomach.

"Exactly. All those things were convincing, weren't they?"

She tried to tug away from him, but he only gripped her more tightly. "They were. I'm sure that you're proud of yourself."

"I even tested out that motion activated rifle outside of Blackout. I have some kinks to work out, but overall I was pleased."

"And the helicopter? That seems brazen. What did that have to do with your technology?" She needed to keep him talking.

"I was just having a little fun. Trying to scare off the Blackout guys. They're pretty fearless."

"But why kill my friend, Karen? Why pull her

into this?" Peyton's heart pounded in her ears as she waited for his answer.

"Anderson, why don't you tell her?" Branson turned back to Anderson, a new kind of smugness in his tone.

"Anderson?" Peyton asked.

Her brother's eyes drooped, almost as if with dread. "Karen stopped by my house unexpectedly. She wanted to talk to me about planning a surprise birthday party for you—in three months. She likes to schedule ahead, apparently."

Peyton smiled. That sounded like Karen.

"She walked in while I was talking about my plan with Branson over a video chat. Said I left the front door unlocked so she came in. Anyway, Branson saw her on my screen and knew she heard the conversation. I tried to stop her, but Karen fled my house. She started to call the police, but Branson had one of his guys close. He followed Karen and . . . I think you know the rest of the story."

"You told me Karen was at home and she'd gone out to her car to get her phone because she wanted to ask me about having a late dinner. That's when she was shot. But that wasn't the case at all, was it? You didn't even talk to Karen's roommate, did you?"

Tears popped into Peyton's eyes as she pictured the scene playing out. "Karen was innocent in this."

"It doesn't matter." Branson's voice held no remorse. "There's more on the line here than just one life."

"What about Suzy?" Peyton continued trying to buy some time. To delay the inevitable.

At least, if she died, she would die having answers.

Because there was still so much more that didn't make sense.

"I told her to go hide." Anderson winced as if in pain. "When I realized what was going on, I knew she would be the next target. I needed to keep her safe."

Peyton supposed that was a relief. But how could her brother have done this? Gotten himself wrapped up in such a scheme?

Unrest jostled inside Peyton at the thought.

"Billy, get the camera rolling." Branson nodded at the guy beside her.

The man reached into his pocket and pulled out his phone. He then held it up toward Anderson.

"You have ten seconds to do what I told you until I pull this trigger." Branson's voice hardened with warning.

"Don't make me do this." Sweat popped up across her brother's forehead—sweat and a good dose of desperation.

He was actually considering *not* doing this? Would he rather see his sister die than own up to what he'd supposedly done?

How could her brother be this shallow?

Betrayal caused an ache in her heart.

"There has to be another way." Anderson's voice cracked.

"You're down to five seconds, so I would get talking now."

But Anderson only stared at the phone and licked his lips.

He said nothing.

That's when Peyton heard Branson say, "Three . . . two . . . one."

Peyton braced herself for pain. For death.

CHAPTER THIRTY-NINE

ROCCO and his guys surrounded the house. Two cars were parked out front, both with Virginia plates. One was a black SUV.

The vehicle matched the car from the video.

The one Peyton had climbed into.

She had to be inside that house.

Rocco didn't know what was happening inside, but he was certain that Peyton's life was in danger. If time ran out or if they made one wrong move...

Just as the thought crossed his mind, Cassidy and two of her officers appeared from down the road. They'd parked their vehicles out of sight.

Cassidy strode up to Rocco and Colton, strapping her bulletproof vest in place. "Let's get in there and see if Peyton is inside. I'm going to stay back and serve as a one-woman command center."

Cassidy was pregnant and shouldn't be in the line of fire right now.

Colton looked at his team and nodded. "Let's go."

Quietly but quickly, they all took their places.

Rocco stood on one side of the front door and Colton on the other.

On the count of three, they would breach the door.

Colton held up three fingers.

Then two.

Then one.

At his signal, Rocco kicked the door. The wood splintered as it flew from its hinges.

The team burst inside.

Rocco froze when he saw Branson. He held a gun to Peyton. Anderson Ellison sat tied to a chair beyond them. Another man held up a phone.

Based on how pale Peyton's face looked, Branson was about to pull that trigger.

Letting out a guttural yell, Rocco lunged toward Branson.

The man turned toward Rocco just as Rocco tackled him to the floor.

They landed with a thud.

But Rocco didn't miss a beat. He reached for the man's gun before Branson could turn it on him.

It wasn't hard to overpower the guy. In three seconds, Rocco grasped the gun and stared down at Branson.

"What are you doing?" An incredulous tone filled Branson's voice. "I found the person responsible. I'm trying to get justice."

"You don't get justice by holding a gun to an innocent woman."

"Innocent?" Branson smirked. "Are you sure about that?"

"Positive." Rocco drew his fist back before connecting it with Branson's face.

The man had already planted doubt about Peyton once, and they'd fallen for it. He wasn't going to hold any power over her now.

Branson went still.

He was unconscious.

As soon as Rocco rose to his feet, two police officers rushed inside and grabbed Branson. Colton had apprehended the bodyguard and already had him handcuffed.

Then Rocco's gaze went to Peyton.

When she looked at him, her knees seemed to go weak.

In one stride, Rocco swept her into his arms. "Are you okay?"

She nodded and let her head fall against his chest. "I am now."

PEYTON DIDN'T bother to conceal how relieved she was to be in Rocco's arms. She let her head fall against his solid chest and relished his strong arms around her as he carried her out of the house.

Maybe knights in shining armor did exist. Maybe those same princess dreams she'd had when she was eight could come true.

Peyton knew one thing: if she had any say in it, she wanted Rocco to be in her life for long after this incident was over.

If he hadn't shown up when he had . . . she might be dead right now.

She shuddered at the thought of it.

Gently, Rocco placed her in an old wooden chair outside. He knelt in front of her and examined her. "Are you sure you are okay?"

"He was about to shoot me." Peyton's voice broke as emotions she didn't realize she felt welled up from inside her and spilled out.

Rocco reached for her again, and Peyton buried herself in his arms.

"I'm so glad I got here when I did," Rocco murmured.

"Me too." Peyton had so much that she needed to process. Especially Anderson's involvement in this.

How could her brother do this to her? Was his love of money so big, was his greed so great, that it superseded his family?

Maybe he wasn't much different than her mom and dad after all.

As soon as they had a chance, her parents had gone off to pursue their own dreams and left her and Anderson behind.

Rocco pulled back from the hug and stared at her a moment. Gently, he reached forward and wiped the moisture from beneath her eyes.

"We're going to get this all worked out," he assured her.

Peyton nodded, trying to find the right words to say. But there was nothing. Just emotions.

"Thank you," she finally managed to say with a shaky breath. "I don't know how you found me when you did, but I'm glad you did."

He grabbed her hand and laced their fingers

together. Then he brought her hand to his lips and planted a soft kiss there. "Me too. Me too."

Peyton wished she could enjoy this moment more.

But the messy situation around them couldn't be ignored.

CHAPTER FORTY
ONE WEEK LATER

PEYTON STOOD behind the counter at her bakery. Life as normal had resumed . . . kind of. Her window had been fixed, her display shelves were filled with every kind of pastry imaginable, and her catering orders were back on track.

This was exactly what she wanted.

Except it wasn't.

She leaned against the counter near the register and frowned.

Her brother was now in jail and facing charges. Branson had also been arrested and a media circus had begun concerning his scheme. Peyton had no idea how long the two men would be locked up, but everyone seemed to think it would be for a long time.

Peyton had often felt alone in the world. But now that her brother had betrayed her and Karen was dead, she *really* felt alone.

Plus, there was the fact that she missed Rocco.

Which was crazy.

She really hadn't even known the man that well. Or that long.

She knew that they had a connection—an unusual connection, at that.

Part of her even missed Lantern Beach, which was also crazy. Her life and business were here in Norfolk. She'd worked hard to rent this storefront and open this bakery at this location. So why did she suddenly not feel complete?

She rubbed her forehead as she reviewed the past several days.

Everything that had happened was a whirlwind.

After Rocco had saved her for the second time, Peyton spent the rest of the day giving her statement to authorities.

She kept hoping that she and Rocco would have another moment alone together to talk.

But they hadn't. Things had moved at too quick a pace.

They had all been separated and whisked up to Norfolk to give their statements to the police there.

Federal agencies had also gotten involved. The situation was that serious.

In fact, Axel had ended up giving her a ride to her apartment once the authorities finished questioning them.

The police had still been with Rocco so he hadn't been able to do it himself.

Peyton had been tempted to wait for him at the station. But, based on the stern looks of everybody there, she thought it was best if she went home.

Back in her apartment, she'd waited.

She'd hoped that Rocco might show up. That maybe the feelings she had for him would be returned.

But, as the days had gone past, it became apparent that she'd been wrong.

She grabbed a cloth and wiped the counter before glancing at her watch. She'd be closing for the day soon. Peyton's Pastries only stayed open until two—after the lunch crowd left.

But the idea of going home right now didn't have that much appeal.

Peyton didn't know what she wanted. She only knew she felt restless.

She glanced at her watch again. One more minute, and she'd flip over the Open sign and lock the door. Her business would be closed for the day. Then she could go to her apartment and . . . what?

Her daily routine seemed rather bland after everything that had happened.

Just as the thought went through her head, she heard the bell jangle above her door.

Oh no.

A last-minute customer.

"I'm sorry," she started. "We're closing—"

The words died on her lips when she saw . . . Rocco step inside.

Her eyes widened, and she wasn't sure if she was seeing things.

Was that really him?

Based on the wide grin he offered, it was.

Peyton drew in a deep breath and composed herself. "Can I help you?"

He paused in front of the counter, still looking as handsome and dashing as ever—especially as he gazed at her with those sparkling brown eyes. "I was hoping to get a cupcake."

A cupcake? She needed to play this cool. "What kind of cupcake were you looking for?"

"One of those special occasion ones you make—the best of the best, if you know what I mean."

Peyton leaned against the counter. "That

depends. What kind of occasion are we talking about?"

He offered a half shrug, tilting his head toward his shoulder. "I'm hoping to ask the girl of my dreams out on a date."

Peyton kept her expression placid, trying not to show her delight. She shouldn't jump to any conclusions right now. "I might be able to arrange something for you, but it's going to take time."

He shrugged and glanced at his watch. "How about in two hours? Could you have something whipped up by then?"

A smile curled her lips. "I think so."

"Good. Because I have a few more things to do, but I'd love to come back then to pick up that cupcake. And my date."

"Does your date know that you're picking her up here?"

"That depends." He shifted. "Peyton Ellison, would you like to go to dinner with me tonight?"

The air left her lungs as exuberance filled her. "I would love to."

A grin spread across his face. "Good. That's what I was hoping you would say."

He reached for her, pulled her hand to his lips

again, and planted a soft kiss there. "I'll see you soon then."

She tried not to giggle, but she thought she might have done that anyway. "That sounds good."

Two hours later, Peyton had changed into her favorite pale yellow sundress. She'd washed her hair again so that the curls were fresh and vibrant. She'd even put on makeup, something she hadn't been able to do in Lantern Beach.

A surge of excitement rushed through her when she thought about seeing Rocco again.

She got back to the bakery and walked to the front door just as Rocco arrived with some peach-colored roses in his hands.

He handed them to her. "Pretty flowers for a pretty girl."

She took them, her cheeks heating with pleasure. "Thank you."

"Of course." He glanced around her bakery. "Listen, before we go to dinner, I'd love to see this place. See where some of your magic happens."

"Of course. I'll give you a quick tour. But there's not much to see." There honestly wasn't. Just the kitchen, the refrigerator and freezer, and a small dining area out front.

"If it's important to you then it's enough for me."

Peyton set the flowers on the counter before reaching her hand toward Rocco. He slipped his fingers into hers as she led him to the back.

It was messy with flour everywhere, bowls in the sink, and colorful icing smeared on various surfaces.

Peyton was going to clean it after she closed—but that was before Rocco had arrived and asked her on a date. Then she'd decided to leave the mess for later, assuming no one but her would see it.

"Looks like a place of mad genius," he muttered.

"Genius, huh? That's one way to put it." She looked up at him and grinned.

As she did, their gazes caught.

That same electricity she'd felt with Rocco before was present now. Only tenfold.

He stepped closer and slipped his arms around her waist. "I'm sorry I haven't been in touch until now."

"I was hoping I would hear from you again."

"It was best if I kept my distance from you until the police finished questioning me," he said. "I didn't want the waters to get muddy."

"That makes sense."

"But I've been thinking about you. Probably too much."

"I've been thinking about you too." As Peyton said the words, she stared at his lips.

As much as she liked talking right now, the electricity she felt coursing through her made her feel more alive than she had in a long time.

"Peyton?"

Her breath caught. "Yes?"

Before they could say anything else, Rocco leaned toward her and his lips captured hers—gently at first before totally consuming her.

Peyton wrapped her arms around his neck. As she did, Rocco's embrace tightened and he pulled her closer.

Heat built inside her, bursting from her core until it reached the tips of her fingers and toes.

She'd never been kissed like that before.

And she wanted to be kissed like that again and again.

For the rest of her life if at all possible.

As Rocco pulled away, he kept his face close and stared into her eyes. His fingers played with her curls as he leaned into her.

"Was that too forward?" he asked.

Peyton shook her head. "I'm not complaining."

"I'm glad to hear that." He moved in for another kiss.

Another one that consumed her and swept her away. That made her forget about all her problems.

Was this really happening?

Was the man of her dreams really in front of her right now? A man who let her be who she was? Who made her feel like she could conquer the world if she tried?

For so long she'd wondered if men like him were really out there.

But now here he was.

He stepped back and cleared his throat. "We should probably get that dinner."

Peyton ran her hand over her lips and nodded. "We should. It would be too easy to get carried away right now."

She took his hand.

Anytime with Rocco would be good for her.

Besides, they had a lot to talk about. Especially the fact that Rocco lived in Lantern Beach and she lived here.

Peyton had to wonder if Lantern Beach might be in need of its very own bakery...

Because she knew of a business that might just be willing to move and an owner who might want a fresh start.

Thanks for reading *Rocco*. If you enjoyed this book, could you leave a review? For updates on future books, be sure to join the author's newsletter. Details can be found on her website at: www.christybarritt.com.

COMING NEXT: AXEL

ALSO BY CHRISTY BARRITT:

OTHER BOOKS IN THE LANTERN BEACH SERIES:

LANTERN BEACH MYSTERIES

Hidden Currents

You can take the detective out of the investigation, but you can't take the investigator out of the detective. A notorious gang puts a bounty on Detective Cady Matthews's head after she takes down their leader, leaving her no choice but to hide until she can testify at trial. But her temporary home across the country on a remote North Carolina island isn't as peaceful as she initially thinks. Living under the new identity of Cassidy Livingston, she struggles to keep her investigative skills tucked away, especially after a body washes ashore. When local police bungle the murder investigation, she can't resist stepping in. But

Cassidy is supposed to be keeping a low profile. One wrong move could lead to both her discovery and her demise. Can she bring justice to the island . . . or will the hidden currents surrounding her pull her under for good?

Flood Watch

The tide is high, and so is the danger on Lantern Beach. Still in hiding after infiltrating a dangerous gang, Cassidy Livingston just has to make it a few more months before she can testify at trial and resume her old life. But trouble keeps finding her, and Cassidy is pulled into a local investigation after a man mysteriously disappears from the island she now calls home. A recurring nightmare from her time undercover only muddies things, as does a visit from the parents of her handsome ex-Navy SEAL neighbor. When a friend's life is threatened, Cassidy must make choices that put her on the verge of blowing her cover. With a flood watch on her emotions and her life in a tangle, will Cassidy find the truth? Or will her past finally drown her?

Storm Surge

A storm is brewing hundreds of miles away, but its effects are devastating even from afar. Laid-back, loose, and light: that's Cassidy Livingston's new motto. But when a makeshift boat with a bloody cloth inside washes ashore near her oceanfront home, her detective instincts shift into gear . . . again. Seeking clues isn't the only thing on her mind—romance is heating up with next-door neighbor and former Navy SEAL Ty Chambers as well. Her heart wants the love and stability she's longed for her entire life. But her hidden identity only leads to a tidal wave of turbulence. As more answers emerge about the boat, the danger around her rises, creating a treacherous swell that threatens to reveal her past. Can Cassidy mind her own business, or will the storm surge of violence and corruption that has washed ashore on Lantern Beach leave her life in wreckage?

Dangerous Waters

Danger lurks on the horizon, leaving only two choices: find shelter or flee. Cassidy Livingston's new identity has begun to feel as comfortable as her favorite sweater. She's been tucked away on Lantern Beach for weeks, waiting to testify against a deadly gang, and is settling in to a new life she wants to last forever. When she thinks she spots someone malevolent from her past, panic swells inside her. If an enemy has found her, Cassidy won't be the only one who's a target. Everyone she's come to love will also be at risk. Dangerous waters threaten to pull her into an overpowering chasm she may never escape. Can Cassidy survive what lies ahead? Or has the tide fatally turned against her?

Perilous Riptide

Just when the current seems safer, an unseen danger emerges and threatens to destroy everything. When Cassidy Livingston finds a journal hidden deep in the recesses of her ice cream truck, her curiosity kicks into high gear. Islanders suspect that Elsa, the journal's owner, didn't die accidentally. Her final entry indicates their suspicions might be correct and that what Elsa observed on her final night may have led to her demise. Against the advice of Ty Chambers, her former Navy SEAL boyfriend, Cassidy taps into her detective skills and hunts for answers. But her search only leads to a skeletal body and trouble for both of them. As helplessness threatens to drown her, Cassidy is desperate to turn back time. Can Cassidy find what she needs to navigate the perilous situation? Or will the riptide surrounding her threaten everyone and everything Cassidy loves?

Deadly Undertow

The current's fatal pull is powerful, but so is one detective's will to live. When someone from Cassidy Livingston's past shows up on Lantern Beach and warns her of impending peril, opposing currents collide, threatening to drag her under. Running would be easy. But leaving would break her heart. Cassidy must decipher between the truth and lies, between reality and deception. Even more importantly, she must decide whom to trust and whom to fear. Her life depends on it. As danger rises and answers surface, everything Cassidy thought she knew is tested. In order to survive, Cassidy must take drastic measures and end the battle against the ruthless gang DH-7 once and for all. But if her final mission fails, the consequences will be as deadly as the raging undertow.

LANTERN BEACH ROMANTIC SUSPENSE

Tides of Deception

Change has come to Lantern Beach: a new police chief, a new season, and . . . a new romance? Austin Brooks has loved Skye Lavinia from the moment they met, but the walls she keeps around her seem impenetrable. Skye knows Austin is the best thing to ever happen to her. Yet she also knows that if he learns the truth about her past, he'd be a fool not to run. A chance encounter brings secrets bubbling to the surface, and danger soon follows. Are the life-threatening events plaguing them really accidents . . . or is someone trying to send a deadly message? With the tides on Lantern Beach come deception and lies. One question remains—who will be swept away as the water shifts? And will it bring the end for Austin and Skye, or merely the beginning?

Shadow of Intrigue

For her entire life, Lisa Garth has felt like a supporting character in the drama of life. The designation never bothered her—until now. Lantern Beach, where she's settled and runs a popular restaurant, has boarded up for the season. The slower pace leaves her with too much time alone. Braden Dillinger came to Lantern Beach to try to heal. The former Special Forces officer returned from battle with invisible scars and diminished hope. But his recovery is hampered by the fact that an unknown enemy is trying to kill him. From the moment Lisa and Braden meet, danger ignites around them, and both are drawn into a web of intrigue that turns their lives upside down. As shadows creep in, will Lisa and Braden be able to shine a light on the peril around them? Or will the encroaching darkness turn their worst nightmares into reality?

Storm of Doubt

A pastor who's lost faith in God. A romance writer who's lost faith in love. A faceless man with a deadly obsession. Nothing has felt right in Pastor Jack Wilson's world since his wife died two years ago. He hoped coming to Lantern Beach might help soothe the ragged edges of his soul. Instead, he feels more alone than ever. Novelist Juliette Grace came to the island to hide away. Though her professional life has never been better, her personal life has imploded. Her husband left her and a stalker's threats have grown more and more dangerous. When Jack saves Juliette from an attack, he sees the terror in her gaze and knows he must protect her. But when danger strikes again, will Jack be able to keep her safe? Or will the approaching storm prove too strong to withstand?

Winds of Danger

Wes O'Neill is perfectly content to hang with his friends and enjoy island life on Lantern Beach.

Something begins to change inside him when Paige Henderson sweeps into his life. But the beautiful newcomer is hiding painful secrets beneath her cheerful facade. Police dispatcher Paige Henderson came to Lantern Beach riddled with guilt and uncertainties after the fallout of a bad relationship. When she meets Wes, she begins to open up to the possibility of love again. But there's something Wes isn't telling her—something that could change everything. As the winds shift, doubts seep into Paige's mind. Can Paige and Wes trust each other, even as the currents work against them? Or is trouble from the past too much to overcome?

Rains of Remorse

A stranger invades her home, leaving Rebecca Jarvis terrified. Above all, she must protect the baby growing inside her. Since her estranged husband died suspiciously six months earlier, Rebecca has been determined to depend on no one but herself. Her chivalrous new neighbor appears to be an answer to prayer. But who is Levi Stoneman really? Rebecca wants to believe he can help her, but she can't ignore her instincts. As danger closes in, both Rebecca and Levi must figure out whom they can trust. With Rebecca's baby coming soon, there's no time to waste. Can the truth prevail . . . or will remorse overpower the best of intentions?

Torrents of Fear

The woman lingering in the crowd can't be Allison . . . can she? Because Allison was pronounced dead six years ago. Musician Carter Denver knows only one person who's capable of helping him find answers: Sadie Thompson, his estranged best friend and someone who also knew Allison. He needs to know if he's losing his mind or if Allison could have survived her car accident. Could Allison really be alive? If so, why is she trying to harm Carter and Sadie? As the two try to find answers, can Sadie keep her feelings for Carter hidden? Could he ever care for her, or is the man of her dreams still in love with the woman now causing his nightmares?

LANTERN BEACH PD

On the Lookout

When Cassidy Chambers accepted the job as police chief on Lantern Beach, she knew the island had its secrets. But a suspicious death with potentially far-reaching implications will test all her skills

—and threaten to reveal her true identity. Cassidy enlists the help of her husband, former Navy SEAL Ty Chambers. As they dig for answers, both uncover parts of their pasts that are best left buried. Not everything is as it seems, and they must figure out if their John Doe is connected to the secretive group that has moved onto the island. As facts materialize, danger on the island grows. Can Cassidy and Ty discover the truth about the shadowy crimes in their cozy community? Or has darkness permanently invaded their beloved Lantern Beach?

Attempt to Locate

A fun girls' night out turns into a nightmare when armed robbers barge into the store where Cassidy and her friends are shopping. As the situation escalates and the men escape, a massive manhunt launches on Lantern Beach to apprehend the dangerous trio. In the midst of the chaos, a potential foe asks for Cassidy's help. He needs to find his sister who fled from the secretive Gilead's Cove community on the island. But the more Cassidy learns about the seemingly untouchable group, the more her unease grows. The pressure to solve both cases continues to mount. But as the gravity of the situation rises, so does the danger. Cassidy is determined to protect the island and break up the cult . . . but doing so might cost her everything.

First Degree Murder

Police Chief Cassidy Chambers longs for a break from the recent crimes plaguing Lantern Beach. She simply wants to enjoy her friends' upcoming wedding, to prepare for the busy tourist season about to slam the island, and to gather all the dirt she can on the suspicious community that's invaded the town. But trouble explodes on the island, sending residents—including Cassidy—into a squall of uneasiness. Cassidy may have more than one enemy plotting her demise, and the collateral damage seems unthinkable. As the temperature rises, so does the pressure to find answers. Someone is determined that Lantern Beach would be better off without their new police chief. And for Cassidy, one wrong move could mean certain death.

Dead on Arrival

With a highly charged local election consuming the community, Police Chief Cassidy Chambers braces herself for a challenging day of breaking up petty conflicts and tamping down high emotions. But when widespread food poisoning spreads among potential voters across the island, Cassidy smells something rotten in the air. As Cassidy examines every possibility to uncover what's going on, local enigma Anthony Gilead again comes on her radar. The man is running for mayor and his cult-like following is growing at an alarming rate. Cassidy feels certain he has a spy embedded in her inner circle. The problem is that her pool of suspects gets deeper every day. Can Cassidy get to the bottom of what's eating away at her peaceful island home? Will voters turn out despite the outbreak of illness plaguing their tranquil town? And the even bigger question: Has darkness come to stay on Lantern Beach?

Plan of Action

A missing Navy SEAL. Danger at the boiling point. The ultimate showdown. When Police Chief Cassidy Chambers' husband, Ty, disappears, her world is turned upside down. His truck is discovered with blood inside, crashed in a ditch on Lantern Beach, but he's nowhere to be found. As they launch a manhunt to find him, Cassidy discovers that someone on the island has a deadly obsession with Ty. Meanwhile, Gilead's Cove seems to be imploding. As danger heightens, federal law enforcement officials are called in. The cult's growing threat could lead to the pinnacle standoff of good versus evil. A clear plan of action is needed or the results will be devastating. Will Cassidy find Ty in time, or will she face a gut-wrenching loss? Will Anthony Gilead finally be unmasked for who he really is and be brought to justice? Hundreds of innocent lives are at stake ... and not everyone will come out alive.

LANTERN BEACH BLACKOUT

Dark Water

Colton Locke can't forget the black op that went terribly wrong. Desperate for a new start, he moves to Lantern Beach, North Carolina, and forms Blackout, a private security firm. Despite his hero status, he can't erase the mistakes he's made. For the past year, Elise Oliver hasn't been able to shake the feeling that there's more to her husband's death than she was told. When she finds a hidden box of his personal possessions, more questions—and suspicions—arise. The only person she trusts to help her is her husband's best friend, Colton Locke. Someone wants Elise dead. Is it because she knows too much? Or is it to keep her from finding the truth? The Blackout team must uncover dark secrets hiding beneath seemingly still waters. But those very secrets might just tear the team apart.

Safe Harbor

Guilt over past mistakes haunts former Navy SEAL Dez Rodriguez. When he's asked to guard a pop star during a music festival on Lantern Beach, he's all set for what he hopes is a breezy assignment. Bree hasn't found fame to be nearly as fulfilling as she dreamed. Instead, she's more like a carefully crafted character living out a pre-scripted story. When a stalker's threats become deadly, her life—and career—are turned upside down. From the start, Bree sees her temporary bodyguard as a player, and Dez sees Bree as a spoiled rich girl. But when they're thrown together in a fight for survival, both must learn to trust. Can Dez protect Bree—and his carefully guarded heart? Or will their safe harbor ultimately become their death trap?

Ripple Effect

Griff McIntyre never expected his ex-wife and three-year-old daughter to come to Lantern Beach. After an abduction attempt, they're desperate for safety. Now Griff's not letting either of them out of his sight. Bethany knows Griff is the only one who can protect them, despite the fact that he broke her heart. But she'll do anything to keep her daughter safe—even if it means playing nicely with a man she can't stand. As peril ripples through their lives, Griff and Bethany must work together to protect their daughter. But an unseen enemy wants something from them . . . and will stop at nothing to get it. When disaster strikes, can Griff keep his family safe? Or will past mistakes bring the ultimate failure?

Rising Tide

Benjamin James knows there's a traitor within his former command. The rest of his team might even think it's him. As danger closes in, he must clear himself and stop a deadly plot by a dangerous terrorist group. All CJ Compton wanted was a new start after her career ended under suspicion. Working as the house manager for private security group Blackout seems perfect. But there's more trouble here than what she left behind. As the tide rushes in, the stakes continue to rise. If the Blackout team fails, it's not just Lantern Beach at stake—it's the whole country. Can Benjamin and CJ overcome their differences and work together to find the truth?

LANTERN BEACH GUARDIANS

Hide and Seek

During a turbulent storm, a child is found on the beach, washed up from the ocean. Making matters worse—the girl can't speak. Lantern Beach Police Chief Cassidy Chambers can feel the danger lurking around them. As more mysterious incidents happen on the island, Cassidy fears each crime is somehow connected to this child—a child no one has reported missing. Cassidy knows the girl's life depends on finding answers. With the help of her husband, Ty, a former Navy SEAL, she scrambles to discover what exactly is going on. Someone appears to be playing a deadly version of hide-and-seek—and using the girl as a pawn. But what will happen when the game finally ends?

Shock and Awe

They thought the worst was over—but they were wrong. When Police Chief Cassidy Chambers arrives at a grisly crime scene, she's shocked at where the evidence leads. Then the threats start coming. Threats against her. Threats that could upend her life. As more clues are uncovered, a sinister plot is revealed, and Cassidy fears the little girl in her care may be tangled in a deadly scheme. Cassidy and her husband, Ty, will do anything to protect the child, each other, and the island. But what happens when they might not be able to save all three?

Safe and Sound

A call for help draws Police Chief Cassidy Chambers deep into a wooded, isolated area on Lantern Beach. What she finds shakes her to the core—a friend is bleeding out, and his last words before dying are: *They know.* Figuring out who killed her friend and what his final words meant becomes Cassidy's mission. Have members of the notorious gang that placed a bounty on her head discovered her new life? Or is someone else trying to teach her a twisted lesson? Elements from past investigations surface and threaten more than one person's safety. Cassidy and her husband, Ty, must make sense of the deadly secrets that unfold at every turn. If not, the life they've built together might come to a permanent end.

ABOUT THE AUTHOR

USA Today has called Christy Barritt's books "scary, funny, passionate, and quirky."

Christy writes both mystery and romantic suspense novels that are clean with underlying messages of faith. Her books have won the Daphne du Maurier Award for Excellence in Suspense and Mystery, have been twice nominated for the Romantic Times Reviewers' Choice Award, and have finaled for both a Carol Award and Foreword Magazine's Book of the Year.

She is married to her Prince Charming, a man who thinks she's hilarious—but only when she's not trying to be. Christy is a self-proclaimed klutz, an avid music lover who's known for spontaneously bursting into song, and a road trip aficionado.

When she's not working or spending time with her family, she enjoys singing, playing the guitar, and exploring small, unsuspecting towns where people have no idea how accident-prone she is.

Find Christy online at:
    www.christybarritt.com
    www.facebook.com/christybarritt
    www.twitter.com/cbarritt

Sign up for Christy's newsletter to get information on all of her latest releases here: **www.christybarritt.com/newsletter-sign-up/**

If you enjoyed this book, please consider leaving a review.

Made in the USA
Monee, IL
06 July 2021